Icon

James Alexander

Icon by James Alexander

ISBN: 978-1-300-12378-1

Icon

Phase One:

Elysium

"I love the way it dances in the sky," thought Rak as he stood on the tallest building in Y23, watching his kite surf the waves of the air. The kite was modeled like a phoenix. Blue plumes rose from the crest on its head and violet feathers adorned its body. Two jewels for its eyes and a slightly ochre beak made it a spectacular sight in the heavens. In his hands rather than a twine or string, a fine laser ran between Rak and his kite. He liked to think of it as an umbilical cord, connecting them. The laser shot out from a controller which Rak held tightly, the slightest movements of his hands swaying the phoenix back and forth. He didn't want to move it though. He just wanted to watch it go in its own unfathomable way. "I love the way it dances in the sky."

A light flickered urgently on the right of the controller. Rak parted his blue- haired fringe to make sure. It was definitely another fighter kite, approaching from the North West. The intensity of the flashing told him the other kite's distance...it was close. Pressing at the bottom of his controller, his phoenix turned to face the other kite. It was a different model, one Rak had seen far too many times. It was a hawk. Slick black feathers padded it and its red eyes glowed. The hawk screeched as it neared his phoenix. The rule of fighting kites is simple, if your string gets cut, game over. Rak turned his hands and his phoenix lowered its height to match that of the hawk's. Both the grand birds glared at each other for a while, waiting to see who'd make the first move. Rak decided to chance it. The hawk's string was invisible but judging by its height and angle, he could guess where the laser was. His phoenix shrieked, talons bared, as it swooped down. Its wings spread, their feathery sharp edges hitting the potential target point. No luck. Rak quickly halted his bird's course, gliding it around and shooting it directly upwards at the hawk. Green eyes gleaming, the hawk released two shots of emerald fire. Rak thought of dodging but he was climbing too fast, so he just took the blasts. He watched as his phoenix's health point levels went down.

"Nearly there, nearly there..." thought Rak as he came closer. The hawk had been hovering in the air, waiting. Rak's phoenix let out a purple-blue blast from its beak. But, the hawk was no longer there. "Where the hell...?" before he knew it the hawk had dropped just below his phoenix's tail. Razor sharp beak revealed, the hawk took a sweeping chomp at Rak's laser cord. String severed, the phoenix gave out a cry as it plummeted to the ground, out of his sight. Rak's controller went blank. He turned to spy the nearby buildings and caught a glimpse of a figure standing on top of one nearby. His purple hair covered beneath his trademark bowler, Rak could almost see him grin from the distance. Turning around, Rak returned to the glowing orange pad in the middle of the terrace, nearly smashing his controller as he walked. "I can't believe he beat me again!" he thought as he stepped on the teleporter.

A flash of colors screened across Rak's eyes. Y23 began to depixelize in front of him. It was unnerving to watch. Then, the scene of the lodge pixelized around him and he observed as other people teleported in and out of Y23 just like he had. Some of them were elated, while others looked and probably felt like he did. Placing his palm on the screen in front of him he looked at his stats.

"Aaawww...no! I've gone down a rank!" he thought angrily, "That idiot! Every time I get some decent ranking he brings me down!" Scanning the screen some more he noted that next time his phoenix would have a lower HP rating. Placing his left finger in a slot, his account came up and he quickly paid some credits to raise his kite's HP back to normal levels. Now at least he'd stand a chance next time he came back. On his right he saw Oliver dematerialize from Y23. Bowler still on at the same crooked angle, he turned to stare at Rak, his dark hazel eyes were stones under his shiny purple hair.

A sneer broke over his face, "That was epic, Rak! I mean, you made a direct attack at my string and then came blundering straight at me! I was just waiting for you to get close so that I could drop and cut you off!" He walked past Rak slowly and put a condescending hand on his shoulder as he passed. "Fighting kites is about strategy man, think before you leap a bit more." With that he got into the transit tube at the back of the lodge. "Ciao."

Rak sighed and took out his link. It was a round, ebony disc that responded immediately to his touch. A translucent light blue screen appeared in front of him. With his right hand he flicked at the various menus that came up. A young woman's face appeared. It was Yui. She looked straight at him with her face arched at an angle.

Her eyes flashed with menace. She pushed away the pink bangs that weren't even hanging in her eyes and said, "Punctuality is important in any business wouldn't you say, Rak?" Rak winced.

"Yes, but I'd also add that consideration and understanding of others circumstances..." Rak pleaded.

"...is not something I care much for. No, it isn't that I don't care for them, Rak. With you I absolutely have to...ignore them or else the mistakes that you've made will probably be even more severe." Yui continued.

"So, I'm late for the meeting with Mr. Lin?"

"Late...would be the word I'd have used thirty minutes ago. Disastrously tardy is more along my lines of thinking now, along with hopeless, reckless..."

"I've got it already. I'm there." Rak turned off the link, breathing out. Yui. Too straightforward, but impossible not to like for all the times she covered up for him. He got into a transit tube and said, "Commerce dome." And he was gone.

In the blink of an eye he was inside the Commerce Dome. Really, travelling in the 'tube' didn't feel like moving at all. It was more like folding a paper, you were just folded from one side to the other. He quickly stepped into the lodge. Each dome had a 'lodge' which was similar to a foyer. People would enter the dome's lodge before going to any district in that particular dome. Touching the screen on the wall, Rak flipped through it rapidly till he found his destination - the World Wide News room. After selecting, the familiar sensation of being siphoned through a funnel ran through him and his surroundings dematerialized.

In a second, he rematerialized inside the room. Of course, it was bustling with the daily exchanges of news from all over their world - Elysium. Taking out his link he quickly flipped the holographic screen till Mr. Lin's location appeared. Group C13.

"Okay, that's close; I'll just walk..." an image of Yui's face came to his mind. "On second thought," he found a nearby terminal and pressed G13. Once again he was teleported instantly to his location.

"Alright, alright...Mr. Lin, where are you?" Rak thought. They'd met before, but he didn't understand why Mr. Lin wanted to meet in person this time. Approaching Mr. Lin's table in the vast meeting hall, he noticed his familiar figure slouched back in one of the couches. Who was that with him? They both turned at his approach, Mr. Lin's familiar red eyes shone as Rak approached. The other man with him was about Rak's height, a bit bulkier, smiling pleasantly. Short, unkempt light green hair and a friendly face were the first traits that really struck Rak.

"Hi Rak! My name's Trent! Hope we have fun working together!" Rak was a bit taken aback...working together?

He looked over at Mr. Lin, who shrugged his shoulders. "They decided you needed a partner Rak," said Mr.Lin.

And that was that. Trent walked beside Rak down corridors crammed with people. Screens overhead flashed news from all over Elysium. Rak's job was to report on crime that occurred in the various domes, so he had to keep an open eye on a multitude of places at one time. The most common area was in the recreation dome. It housed many recreation facilities, so there were often reports of cheating in games, sports, and gambling. The sexual fantasy rooms were especially busy and had reports daily. They didn't actually have to go there, just watch the bulletin boards that pumped out information continually above them and take notes.

"Why do I need a partner for such an easy job?" thought Rak. Trent was pleasant enough though.

"Hey, what do you say we get down to the recreation dome ourselves later Rak?" Trent beamed. Rak looked him up and down. Everything in his mind wanted to make him doubt that he was seriously trying to be friendly but it was also impossible to deny that face of his.

"Alright," said Rak. "Let's finish up here and go take a look."

"Thinking back on it that may have been a mistake," thought Rak. He was soaring through the air in flight mecha. They'd come to Fantasy dome X91, which focused mainly on combat between all different sorts of mecha. He was flying in a different sky. It wasn't like fighter kites. The sky had a slightly purple tinge that made it look like perpetual dusk. His heavily armored plane was decked out with weaponry and munitions he'd never seen before. Lights flashed, switches were flipped upwards, downwards, dials spun back and forth and in general he was amazed he was keeping this steel bird in the air.

"You're doing great Rak," Trent's voice came through his communicator. "Oh yeah, you're getting a little close to the surface, you might want to get some altitude." Too late, the nose of Rak's plane hit the ocean, two walls of water cutting off on either side.

"Aaaww hell!" yelled Rak, pulling his joystick backwards. Suddenly he was pitching into the heavens. There was a boiling, blasting, searing, roaring in his ears as he went further.

"Alright, you'll need to level out now," came Trent's voice again. Pushing the joystick slightly forward, the plane leveled out. Rak felt proud of himself. He was actually flying! Somehow, he could feel currents of air, going past and against him, coming from behind, pushing him along, hands of air supporting him. He thought, "This is what it must be like for the phoenix..."

"Uuuhhh...sorry to bug you Rak, but look in front..." Trent's voice echoed.

Rak turned his gaze from the panorama and saw two large planes approaching. "They're still pretty far. Trent, maybe we can..." Four flares of light shot out from both the approaching planes, heading toward them. "Trent...what do I do?" shrieked Rak.

"Just move!" roared Trent, who'd already veered off to the west.

"Move," thought Rak, "Just move!" he plunged his plane into a nose dive downwards. His plane protested, dials going off the scale and even more lights flashing, trembling from the immense turbulence. Looking at his rear view monitor, the missiles were still tailing him. The ocean was looming up before him. At this speed, he'd hit it like smacking into a rock. Grabbing the joystick again, and pulling it gently the plane began to level out, groaning and screeching all the way. Three of the missiles thudded into the water, which responded by sprouting huge plumes of surf. Rak shot across the surface of the ocean, one still behind him. "C'mon Trent, what now?!" he shouted into his mic.

"Anti-missile flares! Just hit the green button on your right!" Rak fisted it and sent off a spray of luminous fire behind him. The missile connected with the flares and blew itself apart.

"Yeah!" shouted Rak. "I did it Trent!" There was no response. "Trent, talk to me!"

"Rak you should look up." Raising his head, Rak saw a black aircraft hanging in the air above him. Rak reached for his joystick to fire his main guns. Too late. The plane above him had already honed in on him and let out a barrage of bullets. His plane was hit and he immediately lost control, plunging toward that merciless blue wall...

"Aaaahhh!" Rak screamed. Then...he was back in the lodge of X91. He always forgot that they were just games when he was in the domes. He hit one of the walls, "Shit! How many credits have I just wasted?" he touched the lodge's screen and his stats came up. Yui was going to be on at him for wasting credits again.

He could just hear her, "Well in your case we shouldn't really call it wasting as they were your credits. In someone else's case I might have said..."

"Yeah, that'd be just like her." He mused as he wandered to the transit tube and teleported to the hanging gardens. It was one of his favorite places. He'd always come here to just...be. The gardens were high above the multitude of domes that made up Elysium. The domes stretched out for as far as the eye could see. The plants spoke different languages of tranquility to him here. Calming and soothing hues surrounded him, violet flowers, green stems and brown branches hung off the sides of the raised garden walls. The sun was setting, sending pink streaks up from the horizon and bathing the land one more time before going down. He couldn't put his finger on it, but every time he came up here and looked at the sky...something wasn't quite right.

Phase Two:

Malfunction in Paradise

Rak opened his eyes. It was exactly seven o'clock on the dot. Rak sometimes wondered how he managed to wake up on time every day. Getting out of bed, he stepped into his wardrobe and selected casual attire set 69. He emerged from the room draped in a light blue hoodie, beige cargo pants and black sneakers. He went to his desk and grabbed his link. A light touch and its blue screen unfolded. Flicking through peripheral news, he got to his schedule. One thing caught his interest. He was to meet with a person called Xin Yu at 8 sharp in the commerce dome, room A10. He thought back and remembered meeting other clients in that room before and they were always reporting crimes.

"Hmmm, I wonder who it is," he thought as he exited his room. The hallways of his domicile room were usually empty at this time. Most people in this part of the domicile all seemed to work at about 9. The Hostile Dome was huge, housing somewhere near a few hundred thousand people, or so he'd heard. Making his way to the nearest transit tube, he thought about the view from the hanging gardens yesterday. "Aaah, forget about it. It's not like it's anything I can really put my finger on."

At the transit tube, Rak perused absentmindedly over the multitude of dome choices on his link. Research dome, Economics Dome, Cybernetics Dome, Pet Dome...hmm, he was thinking of getting a pet but he wasn't sure what kind yet. Commerce Dome! Tapping the screen the transit tube teleported him to the dome and he quickly located room A10. The woman, Xin Yu, had said she'd be waiting in the Star Mantle Café. He still had some time, so he decided to walk over. On his way he recognized a head of pink hair. He tried to step faster but Yui turned and saw him.

"Rak!" Rak stopped dead in his tracks. He turned to look at Yui, her brown eyes flashing, her head slanted slightly backwards as if she were taller than him.

He scratched the back of his head, "Yui! Well...what are you doing here?"

"Unlike some people who have the luxury of wandering around, most of us have responsibilities to attend to."

"Are you implying I have no responsibilities?"

"I am implying nothing. You have a lot of responsibilities, which is what makes me amazed, no I should say dumfounded that you still have the leisure of going to room X91." Her eyes turned in the direction of the Star Mantle Café. Rak dropped his head.

"The newbie. If you want to know anything please interrogate the newbie. Not only did he drag me, protesting, to that place, but he also subjected me to a humiliating defeat that I'm still not completely over."

"I see," she said stepping closer. He gulped, close proximity to her always made him feel an aura of danger that he couldn't explain. "Of course you know that I have your best interests at heart Rak, I could say it is all for the company, but I really truly, do...care about you."

"I'll take that as a warning."

"Smart choice. You still have 3 minutes before meeting Miss Xin Yu in the Star Mantle Café."

"Right!" shouted Rak and did an about face without saying goodbye.

"I'm dreaming," was all Rak could think as he sat with the young woman called Xin Yu in the Star Mantle Café. The cafe prided itself on its very accurate holographic night sky that continuously moved its way across the ceiling. Xin Yu lifted the cup to her lips in a delicate manner, a small smile on them as she beamed at Rak. He thought she was beautiful. Her black hair rolled off her shoulders, and she had deep, wide blue eyes. Looking straight at him for a while, she then parted her gaze and then connected it again. Rak thought it was like the tide washing up to the seashore then sliding back endlessly. "I am dreaming," continued to saunter through his thoughts before he realized she'd said a lot to him and he hadn't heard a word of it. "Yes, um, sorry can you say that again?"

Not an ounce of frustration broke on her brow as she said, "You see Mr...uhhh,"

"Just call me Rak,"

"Rak, right. You see, I work at the Cybernetics Dome. I'm just like a secretary really but we've had quite a lot of data go missing recently from our archives." She stopped, biting her nails as if rethinking her statement. "No, it hasn't gone missing...it's been copied, without permitted access."

"You mean you've been hacked?"

"Basically, I think that's the gist of it. I don't even know what info was copied or how important it was, but your company has a good reputation for reporting this sort of news and you have access to most of the servers in Elysium. My superiors just want to let the culprit know that they're onto him or her." Rak sat back in the annoyingly comfortable couch; it was so comfortable that he wasn't thinking as sharply as usual. Forcing himself to focus, he realized that no matter which way he looked at it something didn't seem to fit.

"Hacking is the most common crime in Elysium," said Rak, "But all inhabitants of Elysium have a bio signature that leaves traces in any system, dome, facility... actually everything we use here will definitely leave a trace, there's no doubt. So are you trying to tell me that someone who has no bio signature did this?" Xin Yu looked downward and Rak felt his heart jump for some reason.

"I'm sorry but I really don't know. They just asked me to come to you with this news. Can you put it out on your server connections for us?"

"Definitely," said Rak, smiling at her reassuringly.

"I'm sure your Cybernetics department has already sorted out the fee..."

"Yes, that's already been done," said Xin Yu.

Rak let the idea drop, it was probably some malfunction in someone's equipment, once they put the news up there'd be plenty of specialists lining up to look into it. "Okay, I'll get to work on it right away." Xin Yu breathed a sigh of relief.

Her eyes met his, shimmering slightly, "I can't thank you enough Mr. Rak."

"Please, just Rak. By the way," he said, tension climbing up into his mouth like an unwelcome stranger. "Are you doing anything tonight?" She smiled, and then noticing that she had, quickly lowered her head.

"No, I'm not. I...I mean yes, I'd love to...ahh what do you have planned?"

"Have you ever been to Y23 in the Recreation Dome before?"

"No," she said, "I usually like to go to Fantasy Dome X91." Rak nearly choked on his coffee.

"Oh, right yeah, I've been there before too."

"I'd love to come with you, Mr...uuhh....Rak."

"Well, how does tonight at 7 sound?"

"Great," she beamed again.

Rak got up and waved at her as he left Star Mantle. "I must be dreaming," he thought again.

Rak decided discretion was the better part of valor on his way out, and circumvented the area he knew Yui would be in at this time of day. Despite his efforts, he saw a pink head bobbing amongst a group of people right in front of the exit on his way out.

"Aww no!" he moaned. There was no avoiding it, he approached the crowd that had gathered around her, preparing to quickly head for the transit tube. It was then that he saw Yui's head was lolling from side to side. As if she had a boneless doll's head, it flopped back and forth as did her body, swaying around madly beneath a crazed puppeteer's hands. "What the heck?" thought Rak as he quickly approached her. Grabbing her arm, he swung her about to face him. What he saw jolted his heart. *It was Yui.* Her usual perfect hair was tousled and sticking up. Her eyes rolled back and a stream of spittle dribbled out both sides of her mouth as she fell about. He grabbed hold of both her arms and shook her, "Yui! Yui! It's me, Rak!" She didn't see him. Her irises that usually flashed so brightly were replaced with white.

"Noises." she said. "Noises, in the cubicles. Isolated dreams!" Rak wanted to cry, he felt a pain in his chest just seeing the strong Yui this way.

"Snap out of it Yui!" he shouted.

Again she rambled. "Static, static connections!! It's been erased, formatted! The only thing left is...static." Rak had no idea what she was talking about, he held her, as if by holding her he could somehow change her back. She carried on babbling as the gendarme arrived. The gendarmes were the police in Elysium. They took her from Rak's arms.

"We'll handle this situation now sir," they said as they took Yui to the transit tube.

"Hey, wait..." Rak shouted as they disappeared. He wanted to know where she'd be so he could find her later. People began to walk away from the incident, their memories already forgetting it as some strange occurrence. Rak didn't know why, but he had a feeling inside of him that wouldn't go away. It was like Yui had just disappeared, even though her body was still there.

Phase Three:

Static

Rak's hand was fixed on the cold glass window. For how long, he couldn't say. He kept staring at Yui, sitting on a plain bed, sheets and covers strewn across the room, her white eyes staring inanely at the floor, then the window, then the wall, the floor again.

Rak hit the pane hard. "How?" he thought. "How did this happen in a mere few minutes to the most headstrong person I know?" The doctors he'd spoken to a few minutes earlier told him it was a form of sudden psychosis. Its symptoms were amnesia and erratic behavior. They said she'd either gradually return to her normal self, or it could continue for years. These words weren't comforting to Rak at all. He knew that the doctors were trying to comfort him, it was just that what they said didn't make any sense. Yui wasn't there, that was just it. For some reason her body was still there, staring into empty space, but her *being* wasn't there.

Rak jumped as someone touched his arm. It was a soft touch and he turned to see Xin Yu standing next to him. Her eyes quivering, she opened her mouth to speak, then bit her lip. Rak didn't want to look into the room anymore, so he turned toward Xin Yu. She tugged on his arm, so he just let himself be led away.

Rak and Xin Yu were in Recreation Dome H11. Inside the dome, Xin Yu floated in a galaxy of phantasms. Above her head was the Milky Way, constellations and clusters of stars and planets spread out like a canvas. Below her was a coral reef. Its colors were bright and resonating. Tube sponges reached out their spiky arms, waving them to the virtual ocean's rhythm. Table coral provided rest for all kinds of life forms, passing in with the tide, then out. Sea urchins meandered past, lost stars in this coral universe, their shades shifting from dark to lighter hues of purple. Peering over at Rak, he floated above some staghorn coral, his eyes fixed on the star pictures above.

"Poor Rak," she thought. She wanted to offer him some support, to hold his hand and comfort him, but she still didn't have the courage. He just looked confused, the rug of his certainty had been pulled out from under him. She liked watching him, though. His kind face, even though sad now, was still etched in her memory. His blue hair waved in the ocean water like an anemone's tentacles, following the artificial ocean beat. Her heart wanted to go out to him and wrap him up, to let him find some comfort inside her shell. But she didn't know how, she didn't have the language.

Her mind went back to a few days before. She'd been in her office in the Cybernetics Dome, Room R25, Robotics Research Institute. She was just a secretary, but they had her check the cameras at the end of each shift to make sure the security hadn't missed anything. She was doing her usual routine check when she'd seen it. Saying *it* was strange, as *it* was definitely a person. He was covered in a heavy cloak and his head hidden by a dark ski mask. His eyes were too far away to be visible. That wasn't what was really odd, though. First of all, he was unauthorized personnel; second, he was obviously downloading from one of the terminals. The last thing he did struck her like a cold hand. After he'd finished downloading, he just *disappeared.* Straight off the screens! One second he was there, the next gone. She'd checked the surveillance cameras again to make sure they hadn't jumped or malfunctioned, but...there was nothing. Somehow, that person had just vanished. She'd told the head of her division and he'd just noted it and a few days later came to her and told her to report the events of hacking to the news service that Rak worked for. The events at the Robotics Research division and Rak's friend losing her mind were probably connected, but how? They just revolved round and round inside her mind, without a solution. Rak had floated closer to her now, if she reached out, she could almost touch him. Almost...touch him.

Floating in the Recreation Dome, Rak looked at Xin Yu. He was so wrapped up in thoughts of Yui that he'd hardly noticed this girl. Her eyes spoke of concern and shelter. He wanted to run to that shelter. Suddenly he realized he'd been looking at her for a long time and hadn't broken his gaze. Xin Yu's face blushed an adorable red and she turned her head. She motioned to him that they should leave now, as they'd been there for a few hours. They left Room H11, Recreation Dome. It was also called the 'heart of the universe' for some reason. Emerging in the lodge, Rak and Xin Yu exchanged smiles.

"He seems to have got some of his determination back," she thought as she saw a resolved look on his face.

"Xin Yu," Rak said, his heart thumping gently. "Would you like to come with me to the hanging gardens?"

"I'd love to!" she glowed at him.

Trent sat in Room K21 in the Commerce Dome. His eyes scanned the screens above as they continually pumped out information. He held his link in his hand, ready to capture any info related to misdemeanors that came up. The main servers in Elysium were controlled by the Central Mainframe. It was the heart of Elysium that never slept. Every area of Elysium had cameras, voice recorders and was under constant surveillance, so anything that happened at any one time in Elysium could quickly be known by others as it was assimilated and then broadcast by the mainframe to various servers. Certain companies had shares in the servers as information was money here. Most jobs revolved around information or research of some kind. His company LNC, Lin's News Corporation, focused on any criminal activities that had happened during the day. Of course you had to have shares on the right servers to get the information at the right time from the mainframe, and that was his company's selling point.

"We got the news, even before its news!" was LNC's motto. Trent's eyes darted back and forth, as did his hand, rapidly tapping and saving relevant info. Later he'd have to put out all this info on his clients sites. It was quite a boring job really, and he was wondering where Rak was when he saw a man crash into a terminal in the wall. He wasn't hitting it; he was just continually ramming it as if he were trying to walk through. Trent stood up and walked over. Some people had stopped and were gawking and others just went about their business.

Getting closer, he recognized the man. He was Jayden from the stocks and bonds company Hilford and Garret. How had he wandered his way down here? Getting a closer look, he saw Jayden thrashing around uncontrollably. He resembled a robot gone berserk, short circuiting and careening around madly. His eyes were white opals without any sign of cognition. He fell to the floor, not even trying to pull himself up and was mumbling strange sounds. Trent knew the gendarmes would arrive soon; he had to try to hear what he was saying.

He was close enough to almost touch him and he heard the words, "Static...static..." repeated again and again. The gendarmes arrived and immediately separated him from the rest of the crowd.

Trent thought, "It's as if he's got the plague, the way they're treating him."

Jayden was dragged off, flailing about randomly and muttering inanely. "Static!"

Rak had himself in a good position. Xin Yu was sitting next to him, gazing out over the gardens he had seen so many times. Why was it that he felt different today? It was early and the sun shone brightly behind the curtain of some light clouds. Xin Yu's eyes shone too, catching the light of the sun. He moved closer.

He'd definitely be able to explain suddenly touching her hand, "Oh sorry," he'd say, or, "Aaah I didn't see your hand there," or...Xin Yu's hand gripped his. It was tight, but warm. It was smaller than his but the very touch of it made his skin tingle and his stomach, that had been a swarm of bees, became a bubbling, fizzy keg of happiness. They turned to look at each other. They were close, and for an instant Rak thought, "This is all I want, just to be in this moment forever. My heart beating softly like this, her hand in mine like this, this closeness..."

"So here you are!" yelled Trent, emerging from the transit tube. Xin Yu quickly let go of his hand and sat slightly further away. Rak felt as if someone had sliced the air between them with a katana.

"Oh, well..." Rak turned and faced Trent. Trent didn't have the usual Trent face. He was nervous, his body spoke it obviously. He shook, his eyes blinking continuously.

"Guys," he said, panting. "It happened again! Just like with Yui! There was another guy I know down in the Commerce Dome and he started goin' nuts, same as Yui!"

Xin Yu's worried voice spoke, "What have they done with him?"

"Don't know, the gendarmes arrived and they took him off."

Rak stood up, making for the transit tube.

"Wait!" screamed Xin Yu. "There's something I need to tell you first," she said clenching her fists on her lap.

She told them what had happened at the Robotics Research Institute. Everyone was at a loss for words. Trent draped himself over a couch near a clump of magnolias. Rak sat back supporting himself with his arms and staring into the sky that never seemed right. Xin Yu's head was downcast, inspecting the cobbled floor.

"How is this all connected?" she was thinking. "Data going missing, strange people breaking into the Robotics Institute then disappearing, and these cases of people losing their minds..."

"Xin Yu," Rak said intently. "Can we get a look at some older records from the RRI? I want to see if this character has appeared before at some stage." Xin Yu had been expecting this, even she'd wanted to do it, to check older records and see if there were any previous appearances, but she couldn't bring up the courage.

"Alright," she said, "But my job could be on the line."

"It looks like this is something that could affect not only our jobs." added Rak.

That night, Rak lay in his dormitory thinking about everything that had happened. Whatever he thought, it didn't make any difference, and he'd just have to wait until they went to Xin Yu's office tomorrow before they could make sure. He tossed and turned, waiting for sleep to take him, when he felt it. First, his heart stopped beating. He could no longer feel its continual pulsing. He wondered why he didn't feel any pain when he heard it in his ears. It was a faint sound, getting louder. He tried to get up, but instead of moving his legs, his arm flopped over his chest. He tried again, focusing on his legs. This time his head lolled from side to side, without stopping. The sound grew louder. He fell out of the bed, still no sensation, nothing. His eyes were also beginning to blur, his vision was out of focus. The objects in his room merged into one another and he couldn't separate the cupboard from the bed, from the dresser, from the door. The sound was blaring in his ears now. He completely lost his sight. All he could perceive was a blur of color, smudged together. Then, the colors started fading too. He could no longer feel his body, and what it was doing. It felt like he didn't have one anymore. He was formless, without senses, except for one thing. The sound in his ears, it was louder than the world. The sound of static.

Phase Four

Reboot

"Rak! Hey Rak! Snap out of it!" Trent hunched over Rak's contorted body, checking him for any signs of life. Rak's eyes had rolled up, as Trent had seen in other cases of the psychosis, but he wasn't moving. Trent's anxiety could be heard in his voice. He pushed up and down on Rak's chest, still nothing. "What's going on?" thought Trent. "Why's this happening to Rak, too?" He didn't realize that his frantic pushing had turned Rak over on his side. He turned him back and got a shock. Rak's eyes focused on him. At first, it was it seemed that Rak didn't recognize him, then his pupils, large at first, contracted slightly and Trent knew that Rak was there. Rak's body stiffened up, all his muscles clenching at once. Veins popped out on his arms and face, like coiled snakes covering them. His whole body rose a little, due to the tension, and just as suddenly, dropped. His arm reached out and grabbed Trent's.

"T...t..." A parched sound emerged from Rak's throat. "Tttreeennntt." He gradually managed to utter.

"Yeah, Rak! Rak! It's me man. Geez, you had me scared! What the hell happened?"

"C...can't...hea...hear pr...oper..ly...w...ai...t." Rak managed and dropped his hand. Gradually after a little while Rak started to talk again. "Trent. I was gone for a while."

"Gone? What do you mean gone?" he said, hoping that Rak's hearing had also returned. "I...can't explain it. I became, like Yui, and...the other one for a while. I had no control over my body. My heart stopped. My senses deteriorated one by one. And this static sound overwhelmed me. Even my vision, I totally lost my sight for a short time and I was in this world of static nothingness. I could just hear white noise. I couldn't see anything, but for some reason *I* was still there. My existence didn't disappear. Why Trent? Why didn't I vanish like Yui and the other guy?"

"Wait a minute Rak, we're still not sure that the others have vanished, it could be a temporary psychosis..."

"They're gone!" Rak screamed. Looking over at Trent's anxious face he adjusted his tone. "I know they're gone Trent. I can't explain it, but I've got to find out why they are, and why I'm not."

Oliver emerged from the teleporter into the lodge of Y23. He looked around, checking to see if any other players were about to emerge. The coast was clear. He removed his link from inside his black shirt pocket. It was different from a standard link in that it had an extra button on the right side. Making sure he was hidden from the surveillance camera, Oliver smiled as he pressed the gray steel button. To a passing observer, it would seem as if he'd disappeared. However, Oliver could still see his surroundings perfectly so he was effectively invisible to everyone. The invisibility did have its drawbacks though. Its duration was limited and unpredictable, ranging from a few minutes to about fifteen. He smirked, thinking it was the coolest gadget he'd ever had. Eddie had given it to him and all he had to do to keep it was run a few errands for him once in a while. It was a pretty sweet deal! He did feel a bit nervous when Eddie had asked him to copy some data from the Robotics Research Institute. He'd really been on edge that time, but luckily no one had noticed when he'd suddenly reappeared in the middle of the hall. It quickly started working again so he was only visible for a few seconds and he'd made sure to cover himself up well that day. Phew! He'd asked Eddie how he'd made the link but he just kept quiet.

"Aaahh well, I'll find out one day. This gadget gets me into any dome and I don't have to pay any credits. Come to think of it, Eddie didn't explain that part either, how I can get through teleporters without them registering my presence. I still have to touch the screens...Well, doesn't matter. It's an easy way of making credits as well. Eddie pays me well each time I steal a bit of data." Oliver smirked, pressed the button again, he reappeared. Adjusting his bowler, he headed off towards his next errand.

Rak caught his breath when he saw Xin Yu. "What clothing set is that?" Xin Yu flushed a little as Rak and Trent admired her.

"Well," she started, "I wanted to try something new, and some of my girlfriends said that this set was popular with guys so...I decided to give it a try!" She had such a sincere expression when she said it that Trent found himself at a loss for words. She wore a pair of red Gothic boots, white leggings, an orange mini skirt topped by a white short sleeved blouse. Her hair was tied in two long hanging pigtails behind her. Rak had a warm sensation just looking at her, but the reality of what they had to do soon came back to him.

"You look great Xin Yu," he said. That didn't help. Her face changed from light pink to strawberry red. She quickly flung on her white lab coat. "About today..." Rak continued. Xin Yu snapped out of it and took out two round discs. Each disc was orange with a slight indentation big enough for a finger to fit in.

"What are these?" asked Trent.

"Passes." answered Xin Yu. "The RRI is one of the few places in Elysium where if you're not authorized personnel, they won't grant you access." Xin Yu said authoritively.

"Wow, I've never heard of that." murmured Trent. It was true; one of the greatest sayings in Elysium was that everyone had the freedom to enter any Dome or room they chose, as long as they were public. Certain Domes, like the Robotics Research Institute, were off limits. They were generally mysteries, these off limits domes, yet no one really tried to find out why.

"Just place it on your finger when we get to the RRI's lodge. You'll be classified as 'special guests' for the day so no one should give you any trouble. If anyone starts to talk to you I recommend you...try cutting it off as soon as you can," Xin Yu told them.

Rak wasn't feeling right. Ever since he'd regained consciousness, he couldn't get the experience out of his mind. The loss of control, the loss of vision and the static. That static sound that continued all the time. He was also starting to have images pop up in his head, images of people, places and feelings that he had no recollection of. He couldn't explain it. Had something been implanted in him while he was out? Lost in thought, he noticed they'd arrived at the RRIs lodge. Xin Yu was extremely nervous, so he put a reassuring hand on her shoulder. She stiffened up, then suddenly relaxed and made no attempt to remove his hand.

"Let's do this," she said with determination. She placed her finger in the slot that was beside the entrance screen of every lodge in Elysium and was immediately teleported away. Trent placed the orange disc on his finger and inserted it. He was gone too. Last was Rak. He had a strange feeling of déjà vu. Another undeniable feeling he had was that after he went into this place, nothing would ever be the same again.

Arriving inside the RRI dome, he saw Xin Yu and Trent waiting for him. Trent looked really nervous, like he was going to the electric chair. Xin Yu flicked through the menus on a terminal in front of her and selected her choice. Cybernetics Department. Once again, she placed her finger in the slot and vanished. Trent and Rak followed her. Rak was surprised at how empty the Cybernetics Department was. Only a handful of men and women in casual clothes covered by standard white coats walked around the numerous hallways. Xin Yu quickly marched them to her office. Sitting down at her desk she inserted her finger in a hole on its surface and a holographic, semi opaque screen popped up level with her eyes. Reaching out, she once again flipped through menus, folders and sub folders until she came to the surveillance archives. She touched a pop up option on the screen and began high speed scanning for any movement detected in the area she'd seen the man disappear. The screen started to run through the last month's surveillance camera images, screening out registered personnel and was set to halt if movement from any other figure was shown. Rak peered around the room.

There were a few desks here, obviously belonging to Xin Yu's co - workers. One thing that caught his eye was an open screen that hovered above one of the nearby desks. Its owner had probably just left the room. He walked over to it and had a look at the display. It was a diagram of some sort that showed the mapping of each of the servers on Elysium and their connection to the mainframe. Scrutinizing it a bit more, he saw a particular area had been highlighted red, probably by the user. It was the Engineering Dome, which neighbored the main frame itself. The highlighted area was flashing, making Rak think something had probably occurred there.

Trent's voice broke Rak's concentration, "Rak, come take a look at this!" He went over to Xin Yu's terminal and saw that she'd captured an image and was running the video in a smaller window. Rak looked closely. It was the hallway they'd just come in from. One moment it looked empty, the next a figure appeared. He was clothed in black from head to foot and wore a ski mask. He put a removable disk into the terminal in the hallway, obviously copying some data, then faded away again.

Rak couldn't believe he was seeing it with his own eyes. "Trace back and try and zoom in Xin Yu," he said. She did and then Rak said, "Zoom in on his eyes." His eyes came into perfect view. Rak had a piercing sensation in his chest. Those eyes. Dark, hazel eyes. It had to be him! There was a swishing sound as the door to the office opened and Xin Yu quickly closed the window. A man entered the room and smiled pleasantly at them. He was of medium height with a beard and light blond hair. He was carrying a folder under his arm and Rak guessed he was a scientist.

"Friends of yours, Xin Yu?" the man asked. Xin Yu stood up quickly as though she was going to salute.

"Yes...I mean...no sir...they're special guests from the...System Dynamics Institute..."

"I see," he said sitting at his desk. "Please carry on with your business."

"Thank you Mr. Eddie." Xin Yu replied.

"Just Eddie, Xin Yu. It's just Eddie."

Xin Yu breathed a heavy sigh of relief as they arrived at the RRI's lodge. "Thank goodness we weren't noticed!" she breathed.

"Yeah," replied Trent, "But we didn't exactly learn anything new either, did we?" Trent peeked over at Rak, whose eyebrows were burrowed in thought. "Right, Rak?"

Rak's head popped up, "Right! Right. We'll just have to think of something else. I...I've got some things to take care of, I'll see you in a bit guys." Xin Yu and Trent exchanged puzzled looks as Rak got into the transit tube and left.

Trent scratched his head, "That guy. Who knows what the hell he's thinking?" But Xin Yu knew. She'd seen Rak's expression when they'd zoomed in on the culprit's eyes. It was recognition. He knew that person.

"You know Rak," she said goofily, also heading for the transit tube. "Later, Trent."

"Right," said Trent in an exasperated tone. "Later."

Rak headed straight for the Recreation Dome. In all honesty, he was freaking out a bit. "I must be hallucinating or something." Rak thought. When he was with Trent and Xin Yu he kept seeing their figures distort, as if they were figures on a screen, and then become clear again. It was only brief, yet enough to give him a strange, surreal feeling. He knew he'd find Oliver at the Recreation Dome, it was his regular hangout. He had to be in one of the rooms. He went to the lodge and did a quick search of members present in the various rooms. There. Y23, as expected. Materializing on the canopy of buildings that comprised Y23, Rak scanned the skies. Oliver's creepy black hawk was hard to miss. He was nearby.

Instead of picking up a controller, Rak leapt from building to building, searching. Landing on a nearby rooftop, he saw Oliver concentrating on a battle with another kite in the air. Rak lifted his head up and saw it was a dragon kite, one of the highest ranking in Y23. "How had Oliver advanced so quickly?" he thought. That didn't matter now.

"Oliver!" he shouted. Oliver turned to face him, stone cold eyes revealing no emotion.

"What's the matter Rak? Upset that I kicked your ass last time? If you're really that worried I can kick it for you again..."

"That's not what this is about!" yelled Rak. Oliver's demeanor changed from scorn to mild surprise. This was out of character, even for Rak. "I want to know why you were hacking into the RRI's Cybernetics Department's computers."

Oliver's eyes shook slightly as he broke off his gaze, "What are you talking about Rak? A gamer like me in a place like that? You've got the wrong man pal."

"Don't mess with me!" Rak could feel anger rising in his body. "I saw your eyes!"

Oliver turned now and looked at Rak squarely. "Oh, you did now...and what are you gonna do?"

"I just want you to answer some questions..."

"Ain't happening I'm afraid." Oliver removed his link from his pocket. Before Rak could even move toward him, he'd pressed it and was gone from sight. Rak spun about, wildly searching the area. A sound came from the teleporter, revealing that someone had just teleported.

"Damn!" spat Rak, spinning around and heading towards the teleporter. "At least this proves it," he thought. Getting on the teleporter, he quickly teleported to the lodge. As he thought, no one in sight. Rak had a pretty good idea where he could look, though. The Engineering Dome. There was some connection between that Oliver guy at the RRI and Eddie. Stepping up to the transit tube, a figure began to materialize. Xin Yu! She ran towards him and immediately threw her arms around him. Her warm touch permeated him, her fragrance intoxicating his senses. He held her arms and gazed into her shimmering eyes. "Xin Yu," he said, "I don't know why, but I don't want you to get involved in this..."

"I'm already involved Rak. I just watched a news broadcast. There have been hundreds of cases like Yui's occurring across Elysium. It must have something to do with this whole incident." Rak let go of her arms. She was shy, but in the end she was pretty headstrong.

"I have to tell you though," he said, looking away, "I think your coworker Eddie is involved." Xin Yu's surprised face made his heart spin. Was he falling in love with her? "I'll explain on the way," he said, taking her hand.

The mainframe of Elysium. It was the only place inaccessible through transit tubes. The only way to get near to it was through the Engineering Dome, and Rak and Xin Yu didn't have authorized access. Rak rubbed his head, thinking desperately of a way to bluff themselves in.

He thought of a good excuse, "I'll tell them I'm researching news! I've got my reporter's pass, maybe they'll let me in..." Xin Yu looked at him doubtfully. They'd come this far, they couldn't just turn back. Rak placed his finger in the ID slot of the ED lodge's screen. He couldn't believe the message that appeared, "Access Granted." Xin Yu stood next to him and they both teleported together into the Engineering Dome. They entered into what resembled a hall more than a room. Scattered all over the vast hall were holographic projectors. Xin Yu and Rak walked through the gallery of projectors towards a small exit at the back. Before reaching it, Rak saw that one of the projectors was on. He went over to look when he heard Xin Yu's scream.

He ran through the exit to find himself in a massive room. Its dome was higher than any he'd ever seen in Elysium, it looked as high as the sky. In the background large partitions of encased steel towered to the top of the dome. Each partition had a mass of wires and cables that came out like tendrils from the center. All the wires connected to large house sized structures behind them. Each partition flashed and blinked, multicolored stars on a metal firmament. In front of all this stood the man whom he'd seen earlier - Eddie. He held a long black katana in his hand and it was dangerously close to Xin Yu's throat. Xin Yu didn't move a muscle, eyeing the lethal blade. To Eddie's left he saw Oliver, but it wasn't the Oliver he knew. White eyes stared inanely around the room, arms and legs flopping, spaghetti like. Oliver was gone. Rak brought his eyes up to glare at Eddie.

Eddie grinned and started to laugh.

He laughed crazily, long and hard, before saying, "How convenient! How convenient! Who would have thought that you'd come to me?"

"Eddie," breathed Rak, "Just what the hell is going on here?"

Eddie shot him a scornful stare, "You still don't know do you?" Rak didn't answer; he was watching Eddie's katana. "Have you realized there's something not quite right with 'Elysium'?" Rak couldn't deny it. "I guess it doesn't matter. Now that the extermination's begun, it won't matter if I just kill you now." He removed his katana from Xin Yu's throat and pointed it at Rak. "If you die in here, the real you will die too, and that'll solve a lot of our problems." Rak was confused, yet what he said made sense at the same time...the real you. Whatever, he'd taken the blade off Xin Yu, now was his chance. Rak ran at Eddie, fists raised, aiming for his face. He had a strange tingling sensation just above his stomach. He stopped in his tracks. Eddie had skillfully dodged Rak's blow and stabbed his katana directly through Rak's midriff. Rak stared down in disbelief at the blade that ran right through his body. He still couldn't help thinking, as he closed his eyes, "Who am I?"

Phase Five

The Real Me

"Who am I?" There was a piece of solid steel plunged into Rak's being from chest to back, but this was all he could think of. "There should be something," he thought, looking at where the blade entered. But, there wasn't. "I should feel something." But he didn't. Rak stared in confusion at his would-be killer.

Eddie's eyes were wide open, "Whaaaat?" he exclaimed. Pulling the sword out, again Rak had this conviction that there should be some sensation. There still wasn't. He felt scared, bewildered, angry and even a bit elated that he wasn't dead. Why wasn't there any feeling though?

"Who am I?" he thought again.

Eddie stood up and eyed Rak, "Now this is unexpected!" he shouted. "So he actually did it! I can't believe it!"

"What? And who are you talking about?!" screamed Rak.

Eddie lifted the katana and nonchalantly placed it on his shoulder. "I'm talking about you."

"Me? Wait, just who am I?" spluttered Rak. Xin Yu had slowly edged her way to Rak's side. She wanted to hold his arm, she wanted to comfort him, but seeing a blade go right through him had shocked her too much.

Eddie tilted his head and motioned backwards, "Behind me are the five main servers that are connected to the brain of Elysium - the main frame. Unlike what you believe, Elysium is a world in a bubble. Each person you see is an 'icon' of a real one," he gestured with his katana towards Xin Yu, who stepped back, amazed. "The places you see are icons made by real people too." Rak held his head, trying to take it all in, but still felt like his head was going to split. Memories flooded him again. Faces, places, buildings, streets, trees, lakes, the ocean, smiles, the sky and...the sun. The real sun...and a name. A name resounded inside the whirlpool of memory...Ronald Alexander Kingsley...such a nostalgic name. He let go of his head and stood up to face Eddie.

"But you..." continued Eddie, "You're a freak man! Somehow, the real you is gone, but you're still here! Just how did you figure it out you bastard?" Eddie heard what had been Oliver relentlessly hitting a terminal, like a zombie.

"What have you been doing to all these people?" Rak asked edging closer to him.

"It's not just me, idiot! It's 'we' and 'it's' called the extermination. The real you would definitely know. This guy, however," he motioned to Oliver, "Outlived his usefulness, so I pulled the plug on him sooner."

"But he's still here!" yelled Rak.

"What's with you man? Don't you remember a thing? Well, it doesn't matter. At the heart of the mainframe is the mother computer, once I erase you from its databanks, you'll be gone for real. And soon, everyone in this fake heaven will drop off like flies," said Eddie nonchalantly. Rak clenched his fists.

Without even a look, Eddie turned around and started running for the main frame. Rak started after him, yelling, "Run Xin Yu! Go get help!" he ran between the towering pavilions, leaping over wires and cables that were scattered like roots along the stainless steel floorboards. Eddie was fast, weaving his way over the landscape of cords with incredible speed. Rak kept up the chase until they reached the dome that housed the mainframe. All the cables, wires and cords from the servers all ran into here, Elysium's heart. In the center of the room was a very ordinary looking terminal. The mother computer. What astonished him the most was who stood beside it. Trent. He smiled slightly at Rak and then turned to Eddie.

"So...the Front's got some people down here too? You think you're going to stop me?" shouted Eddie. He charged at Trent, katana raised. Two wrist knives appeared at Trent's sides. They were made of dark metal, like Eddie's katana. Their tips curved out beyond his hands and their hilts were at his elbows. Eddie jumped and cut downwards, aiming for Trent's head. Trent raised his arm and parried the blow easily. Eddie took another swing from the side, attempting to cut him in half, but Trent was too quick with his other wrist knife and stopped him in mid-swing.

Eddie sprang back, rethinking his strategy. "Rak!" bellowed Trent, "Get to the mother computer, find your file in the archives!" Trent advanced on Eddie, knives at the ready.

Eddie laughed crazily again. He pulled a link out of his side pocket and activated it. Rak noticed it was the same one that Oliver had. "The only thing that has a connection to the 'real' is the mainframe. It's the only thing that exists in both realms. No one in Elysium can access it now, but I guess it's not surprising you two could."

"Why?" pleaded Rak. "Why could I?"

"Not telling! Anyhow, my link is a bit different from those useless pieces of junk everyone here carries around. I can input data from the real to Elysium with my wireless connection on this link. That's how Oliver was able to become invisible, and how I can create this weapon. Your friend Trent probably has one too."

"Don't listen Rak! Just carry on," said Trent. Rak put his finger in the ID slot on the computer's surface. A blue holographic screen popped up and Rak began to search for the archives. He found them. It was like looking at a photo album, every person in Elysium was there. Their faces flashed before him one by one until his own appeared before him.

"Name: Ronald Alexander Kingsley. Icon Name: Rak. ID number: 7950678."

"Okay, now select, 'Transfer Icon' and keep your finger in the slot," Trent yelled. Eddie started to look desperate. His katana disappeared and a long sleek gun materialized in his hand. "Hell!" thought Trent. He rushed at Eddie, aiming for his midriff. Simultaneously, Eddie let off two quick shots. Twin green lasers penetrated Trent's body as his knives slid into Eddie's upper chest. Both of them dropped to the ground as Rak pressed 'Transfer Icon', and 'Yes'. A window with, "'Transferring Icon" appeared and Rak stared in shock as he saw Trent and Eddie drop to the floor. Then he felt Xin Yu's hand holding his arm.

"Xin Yu," he said softly. "I have to do this. I have to know who I am."

"I know," she said. She pulled him closer to her and their lips touched. It was just as warm, just as exciting, just as wonderful and just as heart breaking as he knew it would be. His surroundings started to go out of focus, as he'd seen before...but now it was everything. The room, Trent and Eddie's corpses, and Xin Yu all contorted, bent, blurred and then went completely out of focus. White static crept into his field of vision, surrounding him, engulfing him in its never ending emptiness.

Phase Six

Phantasmagoria

There's nothing wrong with my world. I wake up at the same time every day. The soft edges of my bedroom comfort me with their familiarity. Standing up, I go to the closet and select my regular set of work clothes, set number 330. I look around the room. Yes, everything is as I left it, I'll just forget about that annoying dream I had. Wait a moment; I've never seen that crack in the wall before. I guess I'll just have to get it fixed. I walk out of my dorm and into the hallway, as usual there's no one around. Hold on, who's that walking down the corridor? Ah yes, it's one of my neighbors, what was her name again? Vanessa? She doesn't look at me as she walks slowly past me. I notice a mosquito is biting her neck, a small black parasite adorning her. Before I can say anything, she's already further down the corridor. That's okay, I've got business to attend to, as I do every day. So, what am I doing today? Oh yeah, my link. I'll just take it out and see what's on my schedule for today. There's nothing wrong with my world.

The link looks different. It has a strange button protruding from its side that seems...incorrect. Anyway, I touch the link and the usual holographic blue screen appears before my eyes. Flipping through the menus, Yui's face pops up, giving me a sideways stare as she always does. For some reason, the sight of her face makes me sad.

"Rak," she says, "Just because I'm your coworker doesn't mean that I'm your personal secretary. Checking one's schedule the day before is common practice for professional insects."

I must have imagined it, she didn't say insects, she said 'people'. "That's why a person like me is so lucky to have someone like you Yui." Yui gives me a flippant stare, head arching back.

"By the way Rak, have I ever shown you this trick before?"

"What would that be Yui?"

"Just watch."

I watch as Yui's eyes roll into the back of her head and my heart starts pounding faster than a roaring, speeding, insane roller coaster. Her eyes settle back into position.

"Neat huh?" she giggles.

"Uhhh. Really...neat," I reply.

"Now get yourself down to the Commerce Dome room Y23 before your already tarnished reputation becomes...foul."

"I'm on it." I say as I make my way towards the transit tube. There's a crack in the wall next to the transit tube. It's nothing, they just need to do some repairs. There's nothing wrong with my world.

Here it is...the lodge of the Commerce Dome. I insert my finger in the slot, but only static comes up. The screen displays white noise. I try looking further into the static, further and further. The image of worms, writhing over one another, made of black and white pixels shows up on the screen. This must be some fault. I keep pressing my finger until finally the selection menu appears and I choose room Y23. As I select the room it seems weird...Y23, isn't that some other place? Aaahh...forget it. Yeah, the same old busy Commerce Dome. Hey... what have I actually come here to do? Yui didn't tell me. I'll just take a look around and see.

"Hey Rak! Good to see you again old buddy!"

I turn to see Oliver waving at me and walking towards me. An image of Oliver with white eyeballs, flopping around and half alive comes to my mind. But here he is, full of life and beaming an almost too friendly smile.

"What's up, you look like you've seen a ghost." Oliver says. "Oh, there's Xin Yu."

Looking at Xin Yu, I feel happiness start welling up within me. Then, Oliver grabs her and gives her a long kiss. My gut wrenches. Xin Yu glares at me.

"What's the matter Rak, don't you like what you're seeing?" she says and the two of them stand there deep making out while I just feel as if I'm in the wrong place.

"That's my boy, Oliver," comes another recognizable voice from the side. Eddie places his hand on Oliver's shoulder while the two continue kissing.

"You've still got life in you yet!" says Eddie, patting Oliver again.

How did things change so much? There's something...No, there's nothing wrong with my world. Eddie puts his hand out to the side and a black phaser appears in it.

Pointing it at Oliver's head he says, "Hey! No kissing allowed in the Commerce Dome, remember?" But Oliver and Xin Yu don't stop, they begin eating away at each other, swallowing each other whole. I watch as they continue devouring while Eddie laughs and fires the phaser into what remains of their bodies. They both burst into flames, and black hornets come zooming out from where their flesh once was.

"See?" says Eddie. "They were only insects anyway." Eddie laughs and begins blasting away at other people surrounding him in the room. I quickly run to the nearest transit tube and head back to my dormitory. I'm shaking all over. *This...*I look up and see the crack from this morning; it's grown wider and more prominent. I'm worried about gazing into its empty blackness. Something about it scares me. *This can't be...*I run out of the room gasping. More residents are walking up and down the corridors coming back and forth from work. As they talk, flies emerge from their mouths, spiders scuttle along their arms, and worms wriggle their way out of their ears. They walk and laugh as if it were nothing... *This can't be real...* Trent comes walking down the corridor towards me, I open my mouth to try and explain the crazy things that have been happening but he just puts a finger to his mouth. I keep quiet as he leads me back into my room. He doesn't do anything, but just points at the crack in the wall.

"Do you want me to...go in there?" I ask. He doesn't respond, but carries on pointing. *This can't be real!* That's right. This can't be real. I walk towards the crack, which is large enough to walk into now. Looking back again, I see Trent nod his head. I go on and jump. Jump into the black, the unknown. And it starts coming back to me. Yes. I transferred my consciousness into the mother computer and everything disappeared around me. White static walls surrounded me on every side and I thought I was going insane in that place. So what were those images just now? Were they memories? Was my own mind creating a delusion because I don't want to face this fact? This fact. Going deeper down into the darkness, the sound of static starts resounding in my ears. I see a faint light in the distance. It's just a speck, a dot, but it keeps getting bigger and bigger. I head towards it and voices start to become audible. Voices over the noise. Speaking words, "Mr...Mr...Mr...Kingsley..."

* * *

The man sat in his glass tower. He was in the penthouse of an extraordinary structure that had been constructed mostly of glass. Of course, the framework was metal, but a large number of the floors were made of glass, enabling you to see other floors refracted beneath you. The penthouse was slightly different, however. Its floor was reinforced concrete too, making it invisible to viewers below. Its windows and ceiling were still the same wonderful refracted glass the man loved so. He peered out over the virgin forest that sprawled out beneath him. The canopies of trees that had watched the centuries change shed green light as the sun hit them. The man in the glass tower took in a deep breath, cherishing each fresh, pure intake. This forest, and many others that had been nearly wiped out a millennium ago, were now thriving. They spread out across land that had once belonged to farmers or where the remains of cities lay. It was a sight that the man wished his father, who'd given his life to this cause, could have seen. Suppressing a tear from coming, he turned to face the long table filled with delegates from various countries who had allied together to rejuvenate their dying planet. The man in the glass tower exchanged smiles and nods with many familiar faces.

He began his speech, "Ladies and gentlemen. Thank you sincerely for coming from far and near for this momentous day. Today you, honored delegates and representatives of the remaining countries of the world, are here to vote on what could be considered the single most important decision in the history of our planet. All of us are familiar with the codename for this operation: 'The extermination', which I personally believe to be a crude choice of words. I see it more as the elevation of humanity through the eradication of unnecessary elements. We all know that only once this 'extermination' is complete can our planet truly be said to have returned to its former glory. So, I would ask you to look at the panel in front of you. Don't worry, your choice will be kept secret from other viewers, but then again, you've come here on orders from your various countries' rulers so the decision has already been made. Please press 'in favor' or 'disapprove' on your screens now."

The room was momentarily filled with beeping sounds as each delegate clicked on their choice. A screen appeared behind the man with the results of the vote. The results were eighty percent in favor of the 'extermination'. The man in the glass tower smiled as he turned and said to the members of the meeting, "Now, let us discuss the first step..."

* * *

"What's taking so long Janu?" said an impatient voice. Janu looked up from his terminal to see the colonel enter the room. The colonel was a tall man, well built, with short cropped brown hair and eyes.

"I've had a few problems, Drew. But it looks like I've ironed them out now. I should be able to have our man online pretty soon," replied Janu, wiping tiny drops of sweat that rolled down his face with the cuff of his shirt. Janu was shorter than Drew, an Indian man. He had a dark complexion, and long, very curly hair that bounced around his shoulders. His eyes were a light brown color. "Okay, that's about it," he said, tightening the last screw on a small tablet computer he'd been working on.

"So what have we got here," asked Drew, much more the military man than a tech man.

"Well, he'll be able to see and hear us, so we can give him the briefing, but we'll have to do the transfer a bit later. The guys downstairs are still busy powering it up," replied Janu.

"Alright, let's get going," said Drew.

Janu turned to his PC. After flipping through menus a number of times, a holographic screen emerged from it. A static picture crackled and hummed as slowly a man's head began to take form. A few minutes passed and colors started to emerge. Blue hair, brown eyes, and a thin handsome looking face. It was definitely Rak's icon.

"Ronald," said Drew quietly. "Can you hear us?" There was silence for a few moments as the icon on the screen gazed around, as if dazzled.

"I don't…know…who…Ronald is…" answered Rak. These words made Janu and Drew glance at each other. Drew took Janu to one side, out of earshot.

"Is it possible that he's lost his memories?" Drew questioned.

"Hey man, in what we're dealing with, anything is possible," Janu quickly answered.

"Then I suggest just giving him the basic rundown. There's no need to tell him too much about Ronald. Actually it would just complicate things even more," said Drew.

"He'll find out eventually though," added Janu.

"We'll cross that bridge when we come to it," said Drew and the two headed back to the screen that flashed Rak's confused, drawn out image.

"What shall we call you then?" asked Drew.

"Rak…my…name's…Rak."

"Very well, Rak," Drew continued. "It seems you've suffered some memory loss so let me fill you in on some details. The current year is 2112. What you see all around you from your screen is the physical world. The place you've existed in for the last few years in your memory is an artificial realm called Elysium. I won't go into its history too much, but what's important is that you were 'jacked in' to that realm all this time and lost contact with the real world. Not just you, over half the world's remaining population are jacked in as well. For some reason you have been able to reconnect with the real world."

"Wait…tell me more…I want to know more about…Elysium…and how the world became like this," Rak stammered desperately. Drew looked at Janu and sighed.

"I'll leave it up to you then Janu," Drew said, standing up and leaving the room. Rak's expectant eyes were on Janu.

"Alright man, let me tell you one trippy story..."

Phase Seven

Retro

Janu looked at the face that blinked on the terminal screen. He rubbed his itchy ear, thinking of a way to explain the situation that the world was in without revealing what an integral role this person actually played.

"Alright, maybe trippy isn't the right word. Tragic might be a better one. Anyhow, at the beginning of the last century, somewhere around 2020, the Earth was in a real mess. The term disaster was downgraded to 'common occurrence'. That's just how many natural disasters were happening, and they weren't small scale. Every time there'd be tens of thousands killed. Whether it was by earthquakes, tsunamis, raging fires, hurricanes...you name it. Well, there had already been a lot of radical groups that wanted to do something about it, but at that time the old governments of the world still controlled everything and they weren't interested in making any big changes. It was about then when it happened. They called it the first 'Environmental War'."

"Roughly around 2030, there were factions of radical environmentalists gaining support by the masses. Their main tool was the Internet. They basically took it over covertly. After that, it was relatively easy to gain support worldwide for their cause, which of course, was a good one - save the planet. Take power back from the governments that just made promises and never kept them and were especially slow in dealing with environmental issues. One of the main figures of the radical environmentalist group called 'The Fact-ion' was assassinated. The truth is that the real culprit was never identified, but that didn't really matter. The Fact-ion used it as an excuse to start their planned uprisings. Coordinating through the World Wide Web they made synchronized attacks on major governmental institutions. Of course, in the beginning their losses were huge as they didn't have the weaponry to go up against the established military forces of the leading world powers. But they had one major asset. There were Fact-ion supporters within almost every military establishment and they began secretly leaking weapons, intel and some large craft to the Fact-ion."

"The Fact-ion had another big thing going for them and that was their support among the people. People had totally lost confidence in their governments and lived in fear of sudden death from disasters that just struck without warning. The governments weren't doing anything about it, so the people rallied to the Fact-ion. The war went on for years. It looked like it would end in the first year, but new pockets of resistance kept popping up and the fighting continued. Eventually most of the world's leading super powers became pro Fact-ion. This was many years later, probably in about 2050. So, the Fact-ion had representatives that held the majority of seats in parliaments in all the remaining government bodies and they started pushing their ideals. The whole planet began a massive renovation; environmental policies were implemented in every nation. Well, the problem wasn't that they were implemented, they became the law."

"It became known as the Green Law. Restoration of virgin forests became every government's priority, creating new ones as well. Natural methods of farming became compulsory where crops were grown on their own with little interference from man. The planet slowly started to become a green world again. For a while everyone was united under the Fact-ion's rule and people were jubilant at the changes they'd made. Everyone's lives became simplified because of efficient machinery that was invented to take care of daily tasks. Eco- friendly solutions for fuel, power and other needs were all developed. This took quite a few years to establish so it was around the turn of the twenty-second century that a lot of natural restoration had been done.

Strangely enough, there were a lot less natural disasters as well. So far, so good, right?"

"This left the world with a new problem. Life had become so convenient that there wasn't much work and poverty started to emerge again in many areas. More and more people turned to the Internet for work solutions and most people's livelihoods revolved around IT or information. But the poor areas in every country were increasing and with them crime and of course - pollution. By this stage the Internet had been developed into a fully operational 'world' in itself. People created 'icons' of themselves online that were made to fit their ideal images of themselves and used these icons to navigate the virtual world where most of the IT and information businesses had all shifted. One particularly great man...let's just call him the 'great man' okay? He was a member of the Fact-ion, and he suggested making a mainframe that controlled the entire net and making it available to those in poverty stricken areas so that they also had a chance of making a livelihood. Now, this is where a rift in ideals appeared. The puritan Fact-ionists were against letting these people join, stating that they would pollute the harmonious online world they'd created as well as the beauty of the planet they'd taken a long time to restore. It was basically discrimination. Anyway, opposing these 'Puritanists' were 'The Front'. The Front basically believed that this harmonious online world called 'Elysium' and the beautiful recreated Earth belonged to everyone regardless. The Puritanists were all out against them. Thus, another fight broke out."

Janu sighed at this point, looking up at Rak's expectant face on the screen, "Hey, are you taking this all in?"

"It's a bit difficult...but...yes...I'm just too...shocked..." Rak replied.

"Yeah, sometimes I can't believe it either. Well, to continue...The Puritanists started to fight openly against the

Front and they had quite a lot of military backing. So it was only a matter of time before the Front was reduced to a small group of resistance fighters. Then to add insult to injury, along came the 'extermination' project. The Puritanists started using their influence to horde people into what they term 'colonies'. At first they advertised them as the perfect society for those whose work was mostly in Elysium. 'Colonies' are basically concentration camps where people are crammed into small cubicles like sardines and given a PC, a motion sensor and a headset. Then, they can stay wired to the net, which is now only 'Elysium' all day. The only time they needed to stop was for basic necessities. Okay, that was in the beginning. The next step was to introduce special 'Life Feeds' which are IVs that provide enough water and nourishment to the bloodstream, and linking the people in the colonies up to urinal and excretory deposits, they made it possible for these 'online workers' to never leave their cubicles. In fact, they started to influence the minds of everyone in Elysium. Through drugs and a kind of hypnosis, they convinced them that 'Elysium' was in fact the real world and that their 'icons' were real people."

"Insane, yes, but you are living proof that they succeeded in their goals. There are hundreds of thousands of people hooked up to Elysium's main frame that never leave their cubicles. They don't have to; all their basic bodily needs are taken care of without them even being aware of it. But recently we've caught wind of the ultimate goal of the 'extermination' project. They intend to inject mass dosages of lethal poison into the people's 'Life feeds'. When they do that, the person's body dies and what you see is what happened to your friends in Elysium. They look like a puppet gone out of control, mumbling and talking garbage. Only some people have been eliminated so far, the ones that were considered dangerous, but their plan for mass annihilation is coming soon. And that's where you step into the picture Rak. Your physical body was annihilated, but you managed to transfer your consciousness to your icon. We're not sure how you did it, but you are the key to helping us stop the extermination."

"What am I supposed to do when I'm stuck inside a screen?" said Rak, exasperated.

"About that," continued Janu, "Another one of the 'great man's' projects was cybernetics. Androids had been perfected quite some time ago and are commonplace nowadays, performing all the tasks that humans used to. But they have one essential flaw, their reliance on a human for maintenance, programming and power. This 'great man' was working on an android that wouldn't need to rely on human control but would be fully automated. He tried everything, but nothing worked. He started thinking, what if a human's consciousness could be downloaded into an android, what would happen then?" Janu leaned in closer to the screen.

"I'm willing to consider all my options," said Rak.

"Thought so," Janu shot back. "Okay, just wait a minute while I download your data onto this removable disc and hopefully if all is successful you'll be able to have a new fully operational cybernetic body later on." Rak watched as Janu plugged a key into the terminal and began the download. Rak had a strange sensation like being poured into a sieve, and then everything returned to static.

Phase Eight

Body Consciousness

What is consciousness? I really don't know, but I've come to enjoy this feeling. Bodiless, the static has gone and I'm bathed in light all around. Waiting in this formless realm, I start to think about who I am, and what I am going to become. I always used to think of myself as my body. I saw it every day, touched it, smelt it and enjoyed the sensations it gave me.

What is consciousness? I never considered that one day someone would tell me, "Sorry, but who you thought was yourself was actually just a computer generated image." My real body is probably dead somewhere. But for some reason that defies everything I've ever known, I'm still here. Of course, I'm not complaining about that, it just doesn't make any sense. When a person's body dies, well, their mind is supposed to vanish too, right? But mine hasn't. I'm here in this void sensory deprivation tank, waiting. That guy I spoke to earlier, Janu, said that they'd give me a body. In a way I'm glad, but at the same time, I feel scared. I lived in Elysium for what...how long? A few years maybe? And the icon body that I had was perfect. It seldom felt discomfort and I never had to use the bathroom, take medicine or do something I didn't like.

Some memories are returning to me. Before Elysium I was someone else. It's vague and indistinct, like a faded painting. But I do remember having a real body back then. It was a lot different. I think I lived to quite an old age. There are so many people's faces that are flashing through my mind and I can't quite place them. Mother? Father? I had a sister too...and a friend, a really good friend.

Thinking about this brings Xin Yu to mind. Where is she now? Will I ever meet her? The real her? All I ever knew was this icon of Xin Yu, a projected image of her. No, even though she was just an icon, I could feel her. Just like Trent, actually whatever icons they had in Elysium weren't really them and the bodies they have sitting in cubicles aren't really them either. The real them...I don't know, I could just feel it, that's all. I should be going crazy...why am I not crazy? I think they're carrying me in some sort of removable disc that has my consciousness on it right now. What is consciousness? It obviously isn't attached to the body because mine is still here though my body is gone. Aaah...forget it, I'll never figure it out. But how did the old me figure it out?

Wait a minute, I can hear voices talking. They sound like an old record playing backwards, but they're definitely voices. And, is that...color? Bright colors, shining lights, it's all a blur and unclear. It feels as if I'm hovering, I'm a kite hovering over this place where my consciousness is stored. Is it really stored there? In that small removable disc? If so, why do I feel as if my consciousness is more? The voices are clearer now...I recognize one of them as Janu's...another, a woman's that I've never heard before. Their voices come in and out, radio stations coming in and out of tune.

Janu's voice, "...I said...his past...don't...only complicate..." It's really difficult to hear but the images are becoming clearer and less murky. We must be underground; the dim lights hardly allow me to make anything out.

The woman's voice, "...still...can't forget...that..." What are they talking about?

"...woman's...surprised..." comes the woman's voice again.

"Nothing...about that. He'll just have to live with it," says Janu. It's definitely a large underground room. The walls are a beige color. All around are what appear to be figures, difficult to distinguish. They're slumped on the floor or laid out on tables. The two people are standing near one figure. The picture's becoming clearer, so are the sounds. It's Janu, he's placing the removable disc into the figure, which looks like a body of some kind. The woman is at a terminal nearby, a familiar blue screen floating before her as she presses and flicks through menus.

"Okay, here goes." The woman's voice said. Rak's consciousness was suddenly vacuumed into the figure before him, entering through the port Janu placed the disc into. Rak experienced a different sensation. Before, he was formless, a drifting entity, a cloud going through an empty sky. Now, he felt boxed in, enclosed and imprisoned. His consciousness began to spread out. First, he felt the familiar sensation of pins and needles and he identified it as being on the top of his new head. Spreading downward, the sensation continued, spreading to his arms, hands, fingers, back, waist, legs and toes. He could now sense his entire body and it was all tingling. Tingling as energy flowed up and down him in circuits. His hands twitched, involuntarily, and he flexed them, wiggling his fingers. Then, his arms began to sway. His legs jerked a little and trembled as he felt their full length. Sound poured into his ears...machines beeping, blinking, the motions of the two people near him, computers. Finally his eyes opened. At first, everything in his line of vision was unclear, but gradually the tiny dots began to sharpen and forms around him all took shape. He could see. He looked straight at Janu's smiling face.

"What do you think Rak? The latest humanoid android, designed by the 'great man' himself. I think you'll find that it has all the normal functions of a human body." Rak nodded slowly, still adjusting to the body. Turning his head, he saw the woman whose voice he'd heard nearby. She had black hair, tied back with a long pony tail hanging down her back. Her black eyes stared back at him. The colors he saw were all so vivid. The girl's camouflage vest, showing her thin but strong looking arms, and matching camo pants struck him with their clarity. She was tall too, and thin, but again he could see she was strong. The bodies he'd seen before were other androids that lay like corpses all around the workshop.

"So, how do you like your new body sweetheart?" the woman asked. Rak could sense the sarcasm in her voice, as he moved himself around some more. Actually he was adjusting very quickly. He tried walking a few steps and they were smooth. He picked up a book from the desk, felt its texture, and carried on touching other things, pencils, tools and anything he could get his hands on.

"Sorry, for not introducing you Rak. This is Chiyo. She's our weapon's specialist."

"Nice...to...meet...you Chiyo." Rak said and thought his voice sounded different. He had some vague recollection that his old voice was pretty gruff, now its pitch was higher, almost...

"Are you sure you don't want to change your name to Raquel?" Chiyo said. Rak stopped and looked at her. She didn't look like she was being sarcastic. Then he felt them. Two weights on his chest. He moved his hands up and touched what he could only think of as two protrusions of flesh that were there on his chest. Those were definitely not there before!

"What...are these?" Rak spoke jerkily. Janu couldn't control himself any longer. He burst into laughter. Even Chiyo, who looked like the serious type, couldn't help but let loose a slight grin. Gulping, Rak placed his hands to his head and the texture of long hair brushed his fingertips. Janu and Chiyo were both giggling now. Could it possibly be that...? He had to perform one last check. When he put his hand *there*, he knew it for sure. His consciousness had been downloaded into a woman's android body.

He couldn't believe it. Was it some sort of trick? A mirror, he had to find a mirror. "A...mirror...is...there a mirror...around?" Janu motioned to a nearby corner. Rak walked over, feeling clumsy and totally ridiculous all of a sudden. It was a body length mirror and he gazed at the stranger who gazed back at him. He had long brown wavy hair and blue eyes. His face could be described as 'cute' from a guy's perspective but he didn't know if it was appropriate for him to think like that anymore. He was definitely tall, taller than both Janu and Chiyo and had what could also be called an 'attractive' figure. Of course, he was using his old self's ideas of attractive and cute. He found himself staring at her...his breasts and stopped himself. "At least they put some clothes on her...me," he thought.

He turned around and glared at Janu, who raised his hands as if pleading innocence, "The great man only completed this female android, sorry but you'll have to make do for now."

"Is there something wrong with being a woman Raq?" interjected Chiyo.

"It's not...that there's anything wrong. I'm just...not used to it...I guess." He looked at the way Chiyo stood. She had a feminine way of standing that made Rak feel brutish.

"Don't worry, having periods and pregnancy weren't included in the design but I think just about everything else was." Chiyo shot at him again. She really didn't seem to like him...her...

"Anyway princess, if you've finished shooting the shit, it's time we get down to business. You've given her the briefing, right Janu?" The word 'her' made Rak feel strange.

"Yeah, just the basics." replied Janu.

"Right then," continued Chiyo. "The Puritanists have started making their moves on the 'extermination' project, which means we don't have much time left. All of the 'colonies' have one host controller. In about a week's time, the host controller is going to command their work-droids that control the colonies to inject lethal doses of poison into every member. The host controller is situated in a controlled forestry area about fifty kilometers from here. It's a heavily guarded place, and a suicidal mission for us. But you're our ace Raq, that body of yours; well...it's special. As you're going to find out. Let's get going..."

"Where exactly are we going?" asked Raq, still unsure of what her role in all of this was going to be. At the same time, she recognized some of the things Chiyo was saying. They tugged at her memory.

"To the training grounds, and you're going to meet our leader," Chiyo smirked. Raq felt a chill go down her spine. They walked down a long corridor, passing men and women, obviously also members of the Front. As they passed, they all stopped to gawk at Raq. They probably knew who he...she was. The android. Did they know that she was a person, too? Their gazes and stares were making her feel uncomfortable. They walked into a large open courtyard. In the center was a middle aged man. He wore an eye patch over one eye and the other one was a pale blue. A purple beret hung loosely over his blond hair. He had a huge build and looked formidable. As Raq approached, she suddenly didn't know how to walk. Nothing felt right. Whatever feminine software had been installed in this android was conflicting with what he/she felt was natural so what came out was a stiff stride that looked totally *unnatural*. At the same time she was having strange feelings. She found herself eyeing the men in the room and finding the way that they moved or the proportions of their bodies attractive.

"I'm losing my mind!" thought Raq. "I've got to get back into a male's body...soon!"

"So, this is Rak?" asked the huge man.

"Yup," replied Chiyo, a sort of 'no big deal' tone in her voice.

"I'm Chaya, the leader of the Front. I've heard a lot about you Rak."

Raq didn't know why, but she found herself blushing.

Chaya gave her a confused look, which changed to one of understanding, "I can see you're still adjusting to your new body. It's understandable that you may feel confused at the moment; after all you were a male before."

"Did you know me? I mean before I was in Elysium?" asked Raq.

"You could say that, yes."

"Tell me! I want to know who I was and what I did."

"All in good time. For now, you need to get used to the special abilities of that body of yours. That's why you're here." Chaya gestured towards the training ground. "Chiyo, it's time to get started."

"Wait a moment!" pleaded Raq. "I don't know anything about this body, much less it's weapons and combat abilities. I won't stand a chance in a fight..."

"You don't need to worry about that," Chaya cut in, "That particular android is equipped with self-learning capabilities. When the situation arises, it will compute a reaction that's most appropriate for you. As the controller, you'll simply need to use your best judgment as to which option is best for you. None of us can give you any instruction in this, because we didn't design that machine. You did."

The last words Chaya spoke hit Rak like a blow in the chest, "I did?"

"That's right. You."

Phase Nine

Messages

The man in the glass tower held the goblet of wine tightly in his hand. He peered at its contents. In it there were grapes grown from vines that had never felt the sting of pesticides. Vines that had sprouted from ground unspoiled by man's plundering hands, the water that ran through their stems was pure, anyone could drink it. Even this glass, it was constructed without damaging any living thing, without harming another life form. "Wouldn't you have been happy to have seen this, my friend?" The man thought as he savored the taste of grapes soured by time's gentle hands. Standing, he walked over to view the forest it had taken so much time to restore. He never grew tired of looking at the rich textures that it exhibited. His mind went back to a time when he was very young. The world had been different then. It had been on the verge of death. The animals his grandfather spoke of had become mythical creatures. He used to wonder what the sight of a whale would have been like, the largest creature on the planet. He daydreamed of the forests he heard tales of. He dreamt of falling around in flowers, drunk on their sweet pollen, picking them and losing himself in the cascade of colors.

They had brought the world back from the edge. The Fact-ion had brought it back, and now because of some ridiculous disagreement, they found themselves at odds with each other.

"Never mind. Soon, our dream will be accomplished. The new world our fathers dreamt of. Restoring the Garden of Eden! Free of anything that would taint it ever again." A beeping sound came from a nearby link. Messages. The man walked over to touch it.

"Mr. Sachs?" enquired a deep voice.

"Please, Joshua, it's Ethan," replied the man.

"Yes, Ethan...sir. I wanted to inform you that the tankers are on their way to the colonies. Approximate ETA will be about 48 hours for the latest one," said the voice of Joshua from the link.

"Excellent, Joshua, keep me up to date on their progress. Take Alyssa with you and double the security at the host controller in the Atanyal new forestry area. I have my suspicions that the Front will try to make a move to counter us," said Ethan.

"Has there been any further contact from our agent in Elysium?" asked Joshua.

"No, that is why I'm concerned. Please also send someone to check on Eddie's situation. Although it's impossible *our target* could have escaped. I still want to be cautious."

"Of course, sir."

The man in the glass tower, Ethan Sachs, sat back in his long reclining chair. Contemplating the future, he drifted into sleep.

"How the hell did I get myself into this situation?" Raq thought as she watched Chiyo come nearer to her. Chiyo was wearing a kind of armor she'd never seen. It started with a metallic helmet that stretched down, protecting the sides of her face, to form a metal vest. Strands of another flexible alloy ran from the vest to her fists, which were gloved in the same metal. The metal strands allowed her arms free movement. Her legs were covered in a similar armor except that it was metallic green. Her feet were also shod in iron. The suit she wore had a panel on the left glove which he saw her flick open and she rapidly pressed a few buttons.

"The first stage is weaponless combat, to let you get the feel for your android," said Chiyo.

"Wait a second alright? Let's just..." Raq hadn't finished her sentence when Chiyo broke into a run, straight for her.

Before she could even react, Chiyo had reached her and lashed out with a backhand. Raq's head flicked sideways from the force of the blow, and for the first time in a long while, she felt pain throbbing in her jaw. Turning quickly she saw Chiyo, standing nearby.

"Okay, reach up and feel behind your right ear. There should be two buttons. The upper one activates your android's self-learning capabilities. The lower one turns on and off your ability to feel exterior sensory feelings, like pain. You won't feel any pain no matter how much you get hit because your androids brain just won't get pain messages anymore," Chiyo explained.

Raq lifted her hand up and felt the two knobs. Touching the first one, a data feed appeared at the bottom right corner of her field of vision in bright red. It read, "Self-learning: ON." Touching the second one, words came up again, "Sensory Input -Pain: OFF."

"Here I come!" shouted Chiyo. She moved with amazing speed, Raq guessed it had something to do with that suit of armor. Again, Chiyo was on Raq in a second and gave her an uppercut that probably would have knocked her out. But she didn't feel anything.

Raq noticed that Chiyo had suddenly gone infrared in a split second, "That must be the self -learning system," she thought. Chiyo attempted to uppercut her again. This time Raq grabbed her fist instantly and held onto her armored hand in a vice like grip.

"Ouch! Let go!" she wailed at Raq. Raq quickly let go and Chiyo responded by giving her a lightning fast side kick. Raq was knocked off her feet, and at the same time her eyes scanned her. The scanning was so quick, Raq just saw a flash of violet. Getting up, Chiyo was at her side again and let loose another side kick. Without even realizing, Rak raised her arm and blocked it. Chiyo stopped briefly.

"So, have you got a better idea of your self-learning abilities? It gets better...if you've fought an opponent once, your android will save all the data about the battle and think out additional maneuvers that your opponent could possibly come up with. So it has its own kind of fuzzy learning ability too. Let's try it now..."

"Whooaa!" Raq managed to let out before Chiyo ducked down and swept at her feet, trying to knock her off balance. Raq sprang up, surprised at her own agility. Coming down, she cartwheeled over another barrage of kicks and landed a front kick right in Chiyo's armored face. Raq was shocked to see Chiyo's body go flying back about fifteen meters. She fell heavily, but Raq could see she wasn't badly hurt. She breathed a sigh of relief.

Getting up, Chiyo looked over at Raq, "Understand now? Your body analyses your opponent's moves and possible future moves too, that's why you were able to carry out that sweet little dodge and front kick. Useful, huh?"

"I'm kind of worried it will get out of control and I won't stop fighting even when I want it to," Raq said anxiously.

She heard Janu's voice from behind, "That's also okay. The system in your body is the same as a human's, so when you sense that you are in danger it reacts appropriately, just like a human would secrete adrenalin and such. Once you're no longer in danger it will just return to ordinary functioning."

"Cool," Raq muttered.

"Okay, let's get on to the next step - weapon control," Chaya's voice said from the edge of the courtyard. Raq looked over to where Chaya was standing. On the wall at the side of the practice courtyard were some huge shelves. They were decked out with an array of weaponry. Most of the weaponry was laser orientated so there were laser cannons, guns, rifles, grenades, rocket launchers and even a few different kinds of swords and knives.

"Come a little closer, Raq and Chiyo," Chaya called to them. Once they reached about halfway Chaya said, "Alright, that's close enough Raq. Chiyo you come over here." Chiyo walked over and selected a large laser cannon that looked as though it could fire multiple rounds at once. She also took and large curved blade and attached it to a clip at her side. "Okay, let me explain, Raq. Some time ago, most weapons became equipped with circuit boards and wireless functions. This means that these weapons can be operated over long ranges without the user even needing to touch them. For a normal person, that would mean he'd need to have a controller which could contact each of the devices and run them remotely. But the android you're using at the moment is different. It's capable of picking up and sending those wireless signals independently. Which means you can operate many weapons from long distances simultaneously. You can also command other regular androids as long as they have been set to accept commands from your wavelength," explained Chaya.

"For example, all these weapons here, except the swords and knives, have circuit boards and wireless receivers. See if you can pick up on them. Behind your left ear is another button, push it and it will allow you to see all wireless devices in the vicinity." Raq lifted her finger and felt the small button protruding from behind her ear.

She pushed it and immediately a message flashed up before her eyes, "Wireless Functioning: ON. Devices in range..." And under it were displayed small thumbnail pictures of each weapon that had a wireless. The laser cannons, guns, rifles, grenades, and rocket launchers all showed up.

"How do I select one?" Raq asked.

"Just picture it," replied Chiyo, "And you'll select it. That's how your android's functions work, they respond to the images you generate in your mind."

Raq focused on the laser gun that remained on the shelf. Then in her vision field she saw, "Item selected." And the image of the laser gun flashed briefly. On the shelf about twenty meters from where she stood, the gun began to fire, randomly blasting craters into the rock walls.

"Whooaa!" yelled Chiyo, "Nice shootin' Tex!" She ran at Raq, drawing her laser cannon, and prepared to fire. The cannon was charging, Raq could see its blue energy gathering. Fully charged, Chiyo let off a single shot. Raq didn't even see it as it plunged into her arm. Pulled backwards and knocked off her feet by the force, Raq dropped to the floor. Rolling over and over in the dust, she was surprised when she arced her body around, like a ballerina, and was back on her feet again. Gazing at her shoulder, she saw that the blast had blackened the area, but couldn't see any other damage.

"My blaster is set to stun, don't fret," said Chiyo, as she let off another shot at Raq's back. This time Raq dodged it, moving slightly to the side to avoid the blast. Raq couldn't believe what she was doing. This body, it was able to sense things at such an incredible speed. Fast enough to avoid the blast from a laser cannon. Raq turned around and made for Chiyo, sprinting. The speed that she ran at was about five times that of a normal person's. She literally bounded. Chiyo started firing rapidly, letting off blast after blast. Raq flipped, turned and twisted herself in the air avoiding each blast and reached Chiyo's side.

Chiyo drew her blade, and lifting it she struck at Raq, who parried it with her bare arm. The blade sliced through her flesh, a deep cut, and she could see the shimmer of an alloy underneath. Not waiting, Raq grabbed the sword, and gripping it hard, the blade snapped in her hands. Raq stopped again, eyeing the shattered sword in disbelief. Chiyo dropped the useless weapon on the ground. She turned around and without saying a word, stomped out of the practice grounds. Raq's eyes had intensified visual ability. She saw the marks left on the sand by tears Chiyo had shed.

"Why tears?" she thought.

"Awesome Raq, awesome. I think you're getting a feel for the capability of this body that you've got now," Janu said smugly.

"Yes," Raq replied slowly, "It's a killing machine..." And Raq also began to walk out of the courtyard, following Chiyo. She had to find out why she was crying.

"Hey, wait..." Janu began.

"Let her go," interjected Chaya. "She's been through a lot...both of them have. There's still a bit of time. Let them try to solve the problems in their hearts."

Raq walked out of the courtyard and into another room. A lot of Front members sat behind PC terminals with holographic screens displayed in front of them. Some of them were talking to friends, others were playing games. Raq sat down at one terminal. Touching it, a screen emerged. Raq logged onto Elysium. Direct access to anyone in Elysium was denied, but she could search the icons. Going through a multitude of faces, some familiar, others not...she eventually came across Xin Yu's image, but she was unable to contact her. The option of leaving a message hung before Raq on the touch screen. It would probably never reach her, as Elysium had been cut off from all contact with the outside world.

Raq began to type, "*I don't know how to contact you, so I'll do it with my heart. To let you know what I can't say. Will it reach you? I just want to feel your warmth again. The distance that you closed between us, has changed to leagues. Can my longing cross it? My heart is wrong for wanting this, but it aches and misses you. Please receive this message..."*

Phase Ten

Narrowing the Gap

Chiyo tossed about in her bed, unable to fall asleep, and her mind leapt back to the past. She remembered that day with painful clarity; it was the day her heart died. Her father was a high ranking member of the Fact-ion and worked hard on their projects every day. He came home beaming at the end of the day and she would sit on his knee, and he'd tell her how he'd been working to save the earth. He'd talk about the new forests that they were growing. Sometimes he'd even take her there. She loved to run around the forests. Her dad even planted a tree for her.

He said, "This tree is about as tall as you are Chiyo. Come back next year and see how big the tree's grown and then you'll know if you're taller." And she did. The next year, her tree, a fir of some kind was about the same height as she was. The forest had changed too. Animals darted around the trees and bushes where there hadn't been any the year before. Her eyes shone as she watched the squirrels scamper along long branches. Birds flittered around freshly built nests and all kinds of insects populated the flowers.

But one day, many years later, her paradise turned into a hell. She was lying in bed, fast asleep, when she heard the sounds from downstairs. Glass breaking, and footsteps moving quickly. They must have been her mom and dad's because her dad appeared in the room seconds later and picked her up. She was already seventeen but in her petrified state she just let her dad carry her. He took her to the 'special room' that dad said they would only use if they had to. It was a locker inside another cupboard in her parent's room. It could only fit one person inside. Her dad shoved her in and placed his finger on his lips as he looked at her. His expression was full of fear, yet at the same time, he was resolute. After that, she never saw her father alive again. His footsteps went downstairs, after which she heard the sound of lasers and her dad crying out in pain. She frantically searched for a handle that could open the cupboard. Part of her wanted to go out and die alongside her father; another part didn't want to waste the sacrifice he'd made for her. So, she just lay still, her head on her knees, for what felt like an entire day. After that, some people she recognized, who had come home with her father before, opened the locker door. Her dad had told them about his secret locker in case this kind of thing happened.

Her rescuers explained everything to her. About the Fact-ion and about how the Puritanists had decided to wipe out the members of the Front. She listened to all of their explanations in silence. In her mind she could still see her father's face as he turned away from her. That resolve. She wanted that resolve, to carry on what he'd started and to make those who did this to him pay.

* * *

Xin Yu walked the vast hallways of the Commerce Dome aimlessly. She lived each day as if it were a dream, days poured into each other, none of them maintaining any individuality...just dissolving into a mass of meaninglessness. When she'd seen Rak disappear and then Trent and that guy Eddie also...she just couldn't grasp the reality of what was going on around her. She touched walls that were solid, felt cold, sometimes warm, but she knew they had no substance. She saw people with bright eyes and shining hair, colorful clothes, gazing at her, talking to her, yet it seemed as though they were parts of a dream. The day Rak had left; Elysium came crashing down for her. How could someone just vanish, without a trace? And before that, he'd been stabbed straight through with a sword, and nothing happened! None of this was possible. What was worse was this ache she had in her heart. She missed Rak. His warm concerned face, his touch that had sent sparks through her body, his kiss that still lingered like an imprint of his existence on her lips. All the people she asked about Rak had no memory of him. All records of his being alive were gone. It was as though he'd never been in Elysium. But Xin Yu knew. Her body told her and her heart told her, he was real.

Later, she returned to her domicile. For some reason, she felt as though he was trying to reach out to her, to contact her. She received no mail, no messages...nothing. Yet she still had this feeling. It was like he was trying to contact her with his mind. Was that even possible? It was a feeling in her heart, nothing more. Although they were a world apart, somehow, she knew he had contacted her. It was a feeling. She sat in front of the terminal in her room. The screen showed no new mail, so why did she have this feeling that Rak had sent her a message? How had he sent it? For some reason, she brought up Rak's old address and started to type, "*It feels like the gap has narrowed. How did your feelings reach me? How can I let go of this feeling, and not lose you? If hearts truly can talk, then there's no need for me to say any more...*" She sent the mail as if into empty space, but at the same time, she knew he'd receive it.

* * *

Raq found Chiyo sitting in the canteen. She sat down beside her. Chiyo turned her head, deliberately not making eye contact. Raq didn't know where to begin. She felt so weird. Here she was, a man who'd downloaded his consciousness into a virtual world and then transferred it out again and now it was installed in the body of an android that looked completely like the girl next door. She also didn't know how to express her feelings properly. She had no idea what history the old Ronald and Chiyo shared.

"Hey, Chiyo. I know that something must have happened between the old me and you. Look, I don't have clear memories of my past anymore. Some of them are slowly coming back to me, my mother and father's faces, a sister, some friends and things, but no details. I just wanted to say that whatever happened between us before, there's nothing that I can do about it now..." Raq recoiled in pain as Chiyo's fist thudded into her arm. Raq thought that she shouldn't have turned her 'pain' functioning back on.

"I know Raq. And even though I can't really blame you for what happened. I've just kept these feelings bottled up for a long time, you know? I'm sorry for not explaining it to you." She ran her hands through her long black hair. It was untied today and her face was only partially visible through her long bangs. An echo of a feeling ran through Raq as she watched Chiyo. The old him might even have found her attractive.

"My dad, Arthur Amano, your old self Ronald Alexander Kingsley aka Rak, and Ethan Sachs were the leaders of the Fact-ion. They were like brothers. They shared the same ideals, restoring the world, bringing back animals from the verge of extinction, depolluting the planet. That's what they devoted themselves to day and night. And then the big issue came up of allowing people in poverty stricken areas access to certain land and also to Elysium in order to make livings. My dad and Ronald were all for it. But Ethan disagreed. He foresaw a regression to the problems of the past. He thought it would slowly become like it was before, people abusing nature, animals and even technology...so he fiercely opposed. The Fact-ion was split into two parts. The Puritanists, led by Ethan, who opposed the idea of a free planet, and the Front, led by my father, who were all for it. The reason I was pissed off at you Raq, was because Ronald sat on the fence. He didn't want to immediately oppose Ethan as Ethan had the power of the military behind him. Also, because Ethan was his friend. He tried his best to change Ethan's mind, but while he was doing this, Ethan pulled a surprise attack on the Front and my father was assassinated."

"After that, Ronald left the Puritanists and joined the Front. He poured himself into research about human consciousness and its relationship with technology. He did a lot of cybernetic research and designed that android you're in now. He decided to go into Elysium when he heard about the 'extermination' plan. His idea was to convince people to unplug themselves from it while there was still time. The only problem was that the Puritanists had already grabbed the host controller. Anyone who entered Elysium's memories were immediately erased and replaced with mundane memories of having always lived in Elysium. Elysium became a world all by itself. How you downloaded your consciousness into Elysium and then out again are still total mysteries. Maybe they'll only be solved once you regain that ol' memory of yours..."

Raq heard Chiyo's voice crack a little. Raq knew it must have been difficult for her, holding these feelings inside for so long. Raq took her hand. Chiyo tried to pull away, then relaxed in Raq's tight grip.

"Hey, can I apologize on behalf of the old me? For not acting quicker? For messing up?" said Raq. Chiyo wiped away tears that just kept coming. Raq brought Chiyo into her arms and hugged her gently, till she stopped crying.

Chiyo looked at her, "Despite all that Raq, I still can't bring myself to blame you. You were never *too* wrong..." She hit him again on the shoulder, much softer this time.

A day before the operation on the host controller at Atanyal new forestry area, Chaya called a briefing. Everyone was seated in the meeting room when Raq arrived - late. She looked around, embarrassed at being late. Then she noticed another thing. The men didn't just notice her when she walked in, they *observed* her. As if they were giving her some sort of rating. She unconsciously pulled at the T-shirt she was wearing to make sure she wasn't exposing too much and pulled her jeans up a bit.

Weird. She never had to do that when she was a guy. People just didn't look at you like that. Taking an empty seat, she smiled at Chiyo, then turned to watch Chaya and Drew, who were standing. There were a few other people seated whom she'd seen before, but had never met. She guessed they were all in charge of different task forces.

"Tomorrow morning at approximately 2 a.m. We'll commence operation 'Shade'. Drew and I have already split you up into different task forces, each one is crucial to the success of the mission. I just wanna say before you go out…good luck guys! There are a lot of lives riding on this…" Chaya said seriously.

"Alright people…" Drew started. "We've basically separated the operation into two stages which will each be led by two task forces. We've called it 'Shade' mainly because the first two task forces are complete decoys. The troops at Atanyal totally outnumber us about 5 to 1. So, the first two task forces will be in charge of drawing their troops out. This is also to minimize casualties as the first groups we'll be fighting are humans. Following up will be the third and fourth task forces." Raq listened closely as she knew she was in the third task force with Chiyo.

"The third task force will have to face the android units that are in the central area close to the host. Raq's in this unit because her body is capable of controlling those droids wirelessly. We acquired the correct codes for their frequency with great difficulty, so we hope that Raq will be able to take care of as many of them as possible by setting them against each other. After that, Chiyo knows how to hack into the host and reprogram it. The fourth task force is basically a backup for the third. If you guys start getting in trouble, they'll go in earlier to help you out. That's about it…if you're all clear then I recommend you get a good night's rest before tomorrow's operation. And please...come back alive, alright?"

Phase Eleven

Shade

Alyssa peered out from the fifth floor of the Atanyal forestry building. At the center of the fifth floor was the host controller. A familiar figure approached. It was Joshua. He touched her shoulder, and as usual she didn't flinch or show any reaction at all. Joshua smiled widely through his thick brown beard. Tonight, Alyssa would get a chance to put on a performance. It had been a while since he'd seen her in action. He gazed at her form in her skin tight cat suit. It was pitch black except for two red stripes that ran down her arms, the sides of her stomach and down her legs. It made her look sleek. She didn't turn around to face Joshua, so he just gazed at her head of thick blue hair that hung down to her waist. Tonight's encounter would be truly...unique.

Raq sat aboard a transport helicopter that sped into the forests surrounding Atanyal. The copter floated a good thirty meters above the ground. Surrounding her were the members of the third task force. They were all dressed in camouflage jump suits, the Front's uniform, and wearing armor similar to what Chiyo had worn the other day. It seemed that the weapons they used depended according to the user, but most had some form of laser blaster and a knife or katana. Looking through a porthole she saw the copter of the fourth task force beside them. In front, about ten kilometers ahead, were the first two task forces. They flew in two transport aircraft, the first with about two hundred troops, and the second about fifty. The transport aircraft were big, but they were capable of quick maneuvers due to advances in powered lift technology. They were almost as flexible as light aircraft, except that they looked like huge bulky birds. The first transport craft would start the battle on the ground and lead the ground forces away. The second had fifty fighters equipped with flight suits to take care of any aerial combat. All the craft were running cloaking devices to make them seem invisible to radar and digital signal processing. The enemy knew they were coming; the Front just didn't want them to know the direction or the level of their attack. Raq glanced at her watch. A few more minutes until the transport aircraft would arrive. Raq felt a sensation she hadn't had in a long time...a knot of tension in her stomach.

Breaking out over the trees, the two huge transport craft released a barrage of missiles at the forestry building. There were two main targets - the first floor and the barracks building at the side. Of course they knew the damages would be minimal, but it would be enough for them to take the bait. The first craft landed swiftly, crunching to the ground with a resounding tremor. The Front's forces sprang out from ramps on both sides of the aircraft, and onto the ground. Their moves were lightning fast due to the boosters under their armor suits. The Puritanists emerged simultaneously from the trees nearby, wearing black and red jump suits and clad in similar armor. Zach, who was the leader of the first assault group, aimed for the legs, arms and non-vital spots of the approaching enemy forces. Though they were enemies, they were still people. The field was full of red and green lines, lasers, neon darts darting back and forth. Zach had a laser shield that he carried in his left hand and a powerful automatic blaster that he fired continually in his right. He blocked blasts while firing, watching as the much larger force of Puritanists advanced, gaining ground. Raising his hand, he made a v-shaped signal with his fingers. As his men saw it, they continued firing, while retreating into the forest thicket behind them.

At the same time, from the second craft, Front fighters wearing flight suits emerged. Flight suits were basically the same as armor, but they were adapted around a central core with a pack on the back. They used the same principle as turbo jet packs to fly. The suits had nozzles that blasted jets of air under the arms and feet, so they could keep the pilot flying and move in almost any direction. They also had arm handles, equipped with powerful laser blasters under each arm and a few short range missiles on the pack. The Flight suits flew up towards the roof of the Atanyal building. As expected, there were a large number of enemy flight suits and a few aircraft on the roof. The Front's forces shot off blasts into the ranks of Puritanists. Flight suits blazed, flames licking up their metal skins and others fell over, struck by piercing blasts. They returned fire and some of the Front's fighters dropped from the air. The leader of the group, Drew, signaled for the pilots to ascend further into the air. They all began to rise higher and higher. The Puritanists responded by taking to the air as well, except the aircraft, which still remained motionless on the roof.

As the two battles flared up on both sides, the third task force slipped over the tops of the trees and landed outside Atanyal. Raq jumped out of the chopper, followed by Chiyo and a force of about twenty-three troopers. They stormed the entrance and then came to a halt. Chiyo motioned for them to stay back as Raq barged through the glass doors. Raq wasn't wearing armor, her body was sufficient. As soon as she entered the first floor, wireless signals from about fifteen androids flickered in her line of vision. Before she could do anything, a red shot seared through the air toward her. Stretching her body over backwards, the laser burnt through the material of her jump suit, narrowly missing.

"This is going to be difficult," Raq mused. "They're using the darkness to their advantage here, and if they keep shooting, I won't be able to focus for long enough to connect with their signals." A red thumbnail popped up at the bottom of her sight, 'Night Vision'. Quickly selecting it, her targets came into sight. Human shaped machines, moving slowly towards her. More shots leapt from their weapons towards her. Something sliced through her leg, but she didn't feel it. She started to run, straight at them, her speed making them miss. As she approached, she unsheathed a long curved katana that had been strapped on her back. Dancing through their midst, she struck out at them. Aiming for their weak points, she took out their eyes. Reaching the wall, she ran up it, her sheer speed enabling her to run along the wall. Again, the androids fired at her, and she threaded her way through the barrage. Coming down the other side of the room, she crouched behind a pillar. Quickly she traced their signals, locking onto each one. Then, computing quickly, she had them target each other. Just as a male android leapt out in front of her she selected, 'initiate'. The android let off one blast, which struck the pillar beside her, before turning his eyes toward the other androids. He started shooting randomly at any other androids that he could. The others were doing the same. Peering out from behind the pillar, Raq breathed a sigh of relief as she saw all the androids blasting each other to pieces.

Zach clutched his arm, an intense, burning pain rising from the laser wound. He dropped his shield, he couldn't hold onto it now. His right arm was still good, so he continued firing and withdrawing deeper into the forest. Around him, the carnage was unbelievable. The night air was alight with laser blasts, deadly fireworks spurting between men and women. Screams filled his ears, screams that he could do nothing about. Injured troops lay all over the forest's floor. Some of them were motionless, their lack of motion was an even harsher blow to him. The enemy outnumbered them way too much. They were going to be wiped out, if something didn't happen, soon.

Drew aimed at the Puritanist in front of him and let off a strong shot. It clipped the man in front of him, and he lost control of his flight suit. Screaming out in fear, he dropped to the harsh ground. Moving quick, Drew evaded fire that was coming from his flank. Rapid fire, spurts of green death, rained down and one of his troopers was caught in it. The blast penetrated his head, blood spurting out the back of his skull.

The trooper stopped momentarily, the way a hummingbird does, hovering, before he plunged down to the dust. Drew's anger flared up. Boosting himself up, he came to the same level as the attacker. His artillery was quite different to anything Drew had seen before. His flight suit was equipped with a laser cannon that had a revolving barrel, it could let off a long series of blasts without recharging. The man in the suit wasn't wearing a helmet, and a pair of remorseless pale blue eyes stared back at him. The man grinned slightly, zoning in on Drew. "Bye," the man said as he started to let off a round of shots. Drew cut his jets and sank like a stone, green lights flashing overhead. Then, after dropping about twenty meters, he flipped the boosters back on and shot up at an angle, releasing his missiles. He stopped and gazed up as the missile connected with the Puritanist's suit. He saw those pale blue eyes widen, this time afraid. A globe of fire encased him and he let out a last frantic round of aimless blasts, before tumbling down.

"Yeah...bye," murmured Drew.

Inside the building Raq climbed the escape stairs to the second floor, while Chiyo moved in with her forces to secure the first. Before even reaching the second floor she detected the androids on that level. Once again she set them against each other. Emerging on the second floor, it was already a battlefield as brainwashed androids blasted and cut away at their comrades. The same thing happened on the third and fourth floor. Bolting up the last set of stairs, Raq was surprised to detect no wireless androids in range.

"That's weird," she thought. "The most important level is either unprotected or protected only by humans. If it is people it'll make this a lot more difficult, but I've still gotta do it." She scaled the last flight of stairs and emerged on the fifth floor. Eyes darting around, she immediately scanned the area. Two presences were visible in the center of the room. Lighting was normal, so she used her telescopic vision to zoom in on them. The one was a woman, tall, with blue hair and wearing a black cat suit with red stripes. The other was a middle aged man, with wavy hair and a thick beard. He wore the Puritansits' uniform. They were both approaching Raq from the middle of the room. Raq scanned again for weapons, detecting a handheld laser gun in the man's hand, and a laser cannon slung over the girls shoulder. Raq decided not to make a move but to assess them first. Scrutinizing closer, she saw the woman was definitely an android, the man human. Something was familiar about them but she couldn't put her finger on it.

When they were in close enough range Raq decided not to wait anymore.

Then the man spoke, "Well, well. If it isn't the Y-23 model. Ronald finally completed it. And to see it moving around can only mean one thing. You're in there aren't you Ronald?" His words surprised Raq, how could he know she had been Ronald before...and how much did he know?

"What do you know about me?" Raq yelled at him.

"You used to be my commanding officer. I watched you begin crafting that Y-23 model, before you deserted us and went to the Front. One thing I remember clearly though was you stating that it would only be possible to download your consciousness into it. At the time I thought you were just a mad scientist...now I'm really intrigued as to how you did it," replied Joshua.

"That's something you won't be finding out!" yelled Raq, gritting her teeth.

"Oh, yes how rude of me. Ronald, the first human android, meet Alyssa, the first android to ever gain consciousness," said Joshua in an irritating tone.

"Gain consciousness? An android?" Raq asked.

"Yes, she's quite unique among androids. From her creation till now I've watched her, and she displays behavior that other androids never do. Most androids are just that, machines. But Alyssa started to display human like qualities from the beginning. Caring for plants without our asking, working with sick or injured animals. She even maintains her android companions, though they don't show her the slightest reaction. She's even quite popular among the troops for talking to them and showing concern for them. She wouldn't show up on your wireless detector as she's an independent unit. Just like you are," smirked Joshua. His enjoyment of all this was irking Raq.

"Anyway, I suppose you're here for this," he motioned at the host controller in the center of the room. "Your timing is really perfect. I was just about to start the program that will command the worker droids on the colonies to inject their inhabitants 'Life Feeds' with lethal poison. It's wonderful that you can be here for this moment Ronald."

Raq stared Joshua directly in the eyes. "It's not Ronald. It's Raq!" With that, she sped toward Joshua, ready to slice him with her katana. Twirling to his side, she plunged the sword towards his arm, hoping to disable him. Another blade appeared before hers, blocking Joshua. She struck down on it full force and felt her own blade shudder in her hands. It was Alyssa, touching a button on the side of the blade, Alyssa's sword crackled with an electric current. Raq was jolted by the shock and flew backwards, slamming into the wall.

Raq stood up, staring at her strange opponent. She had the appearance of an android, not as perfectly human-like as her own so more easily noticeable. Her red eyes glared back at Raq. Raq almost felt sad that she had to fight her; in a way she felt that they were kindred spirits. Nonetheless, she locked on to the laser cannon attached to Alyssa's back and began firing the weapon. The barrel was pointed downwards, so the blaster let loose a barrage at the ground below Alyssa. Chips of rock flew up from the marble floor scattering debris all over. Alyssa's leg was hit, but she showed no pain. Reaching back, she withdrew the blaster from its holster and threw it against the wall, still spraying lasers as it snapped in two. They squared off, eyeing the other, blades in hand. Without a sound, Alyssa rolled at Raq. Caught off guard and not computing her attacks, Raq was bowled over and went headfirst to the ground. The impact would have knocked a person out. Raq decided to make use of the opportunity and got up to head for the real source of the problem, the man controlling her.

Dashing, in one bound she was at his side. But Allyssa somersaulted over her head to stand in front of Joshua. Alyssa thrust out, and Raq brought up her blade to block, quickly pushing it aside before Alyssa could send a current through it.

"The self-learning system must be kicking in," Raq thought. Again, Alyssa struck with a sideways slice and Raq decided to chance it. She grabbed the blade, which cut deep into her synthetic skin and grated against the metal alloy underneath. Then bringing her leg up, she gave Alyssa a frontal kick in the stomach, sending her flying back. Taking Alyssa's sword in both hands, she snapped it in two, then quickly turned to face the man, but he'd disappeared. Hurriedly examining the area for his presence, she noted that he was nearby the host controller. She immediately darted for him, forgetting about the fallen Alyssa.

"Just a bit more..." thought Raq. As she darted along the floor, Alyssa grabbed one of her legs. Raq dug her heel into the ground to stop her motion and swung the other to connect with Alyssa face. The ball of her foot connected directly under Alyssa jaw, but not before Alyssa stabbed a hand knife into Raq's side. Alyssa's head released sparks from the blow's impact and she sprawled back a few feet. Raq put her hand to her side to pull out the knife, and then noticed where she'd been stabbed.

The blade was neatly inserted into the area where her memory was stored on the removable disc. She watched as it frizzled slightly. The disc was obviously destroyed. Raq's vision began to grow dim, the lights in her eyes became fainter and fainter...until she stood motionless on the fifth floor of Atanyal. Her eyes were completely dark; no sign of life could be seen.

Phase Twelve

Electronic Soul

"The situation isn't looking good here," Zach's voice crackled on Chiyo's earpiece. "Severely outnumbered...heavy losses...need to evacuate soon..."

"Damn! Lost his signal!" thought Chiyo, praying Zach was still alive. More crackling entered her ears.

"Chiyo, this is Drew. We're holding up alright. We've taken out quite a few of their flight suits and one of the aircraft on the roof. Hurry up in there! We need to get help to the forces on the ground," Drew's voice came through.

Chiyo gritted her teeth and ascended to the fifth floor. She couldn't believe what she saw. About twenty meters from her was an android's body, laying unconscious on the floor. Nearby, Raq stood like a statue. She didn't move. Her eyes were wide open but no light shone from within them as they usually did. Chiyo wondered what had happened here and observed Raq closer. She saw a wound in her side, right where Janu had installed her memory disc. Could it be? She heard sounds from behind her. Her troops were arriving behind her. They quickly entered the room and Chiyo headed towards Raq. As she ran, she saw the host controller in the center of the large room. It was a huge super computer. Massive locker like cases housed the hardware of the host, whereas the terminal was somewhere near the middle. Running past Raq, she knew she had to get to that terminal quickly. Passing a few towers filled with electronic equipment, she came to the center. There at the terminal, was an all too familiar figure...Joshua. He was entering something on the screen and didn't even look up. Chiyo rapidly drew her blaster. At her movement, Joshua leapt away from the screen. She didn't dare fire now, in case she hit some part of the main frame. Joshua was crawling towards a nearby staircase, she figured it went up to the roof. But as she was passing the terminal screen, she saw a command being executed. 'Initializing Command: Extermination', and it was about 20% finished. Forgetting Joshua, she dropped her blaster and pulled out the terminal's keyboard. Typing frantically, she attempted to crack the command's code before it initialized.

0110110110110110111000110000110101001101001110011000110101110011011010011 Raq swam in a sea of binary. Commands and languages washed over her. Expressions, atoms, numbers, symbols, the language of the machine. Executions and applications, the heart of the machine. In here, Raq was reduced to nothing more than data. Data. A smiling boy with curly hair playing on the sand, mom and dad watching, waves of blue crashing in the poignant background. Data. A man holding a small baby seal in his hands, gun to its head, precious white fur greed-red on white snow. Data. Trees falling, earth shaking, fire bellowing from the earth's guts, walls so high, toy cars bobbing, pulling away the last slab the child cries. Data. The rapid fire of guns emptying their minds and they scream as another rips through the peaceful night's moon...soaked in the sounds.

I am Ronald Alexander Kingsley. I was born to Martha and George Kingsley. I had a sister, Grace Kingsley. I grew up in a world divided by war. People fighting against those they said didn't care about them, didn't care about the world. So, I fought too. I picked up the banner of the Fact-ion's cause and we won. Every day was like a dream come true. Every day I touched people. I touched people who'd been starving, and gave them meals. I sought animals that were nearly gone and brought them back. I went to green worlds that were decimated, and started to replant them. Smiling, with dirty brown hands and honest sweat. Then, it came back, the greed I'd seen before. The man who I'd walked with, shared my ideals with, and laughed with...became my enemy. So, I walked away. I did something, I found some way to get out of the prison, and I entered a new world.

I remember Elysium. I became Rak. I remember Yui's reprimanding, concerned face. I remember Trent's sincere stare, Xin Yu's big ocean wide eyes. I remember living in a fantasy world that couldn't last. I came out and entered a home that I'd prepared. A body that I'd made for myself, Raq. To finish what I'd started. Yes, to finish what I started. So why do I remember all this? The disc was destroyed. It contained everything...my existence, my memories. It was the testimony that I was alive, a living creature. Now though, I'm nothing but binary and numbers and...no...Memories in the human body aren't only stored in the brain. There were theories that the body itself retained memories. So what if...let me see...yes. There it is...my arm. Now, my leg, my hands, my feet...my eyes...

Raq's eyes suddenly opened wide, color returned to them and her body started to move. How? Oh yes, her memories had already spread themselves throughout the nervous system and even into her artificial brain. The memory disc was basically like a temporary storage until Raq's consciousness had fused with her new body. Turning, it all came back to her. The battle, the android Alyssa had stabbed her; she still lay there on the floor like a rag doll. Raq turned and got moving towards the host controller. Making her way through the main frame, she reached the central terminal to find Chiyo typing frantically on the keys. She was trying to deactivate the programs that had been set in motion to poison all the inhabitants of the colonies. Chiyo stared up at Raq as she approached, a look of relief washing over her face.

"Raq, please do something, I can't stop this program, I just don't..." Chiyo said frantically.

"I'll do it," Raq cut in and placed her finger in the I.D. slot. An option to 'Terminate Extermination Program' came up and Raq selected it. The progress box disappeared and Chiyo slumped down on the floor.

"Jeez, why didn't you come sooner? I was going nuts there," Chiyo complained.

Raq noticed the staircase going upwards and said, "My bad. What about Joshua?"

"Probably long gone on one of the airplanes...the spineless wimp."

"I see," Raq responded. Touching the miniature mic on her collar, Raq tried contacting Zach, but got no response. She tried again with Drew, and got through.

"Drew, what's your status?" asked Raq urgently.

"We're down to about ten flight suits, but most of the enemies that were in the air have been wiped out and some high tailed it. What's your plan Raq?"

Raq emerged on the rooftop with Chiyo close behind. There were about thirty flight suits and a fighter jet on the roof. "I'm going to take control of these suits. We're going to bail Zach out," Raq said.

"Sounds good to me," replied Drew.

Joshua piloted the aircraft smoothly back to the Puritanists' base. The base was at the building called 'Procerus'. It was made almost entirely of strong reinforced glass with only the top having a concrete floor. Beside the towering monolith were hangars that housed more than a hundred aircraft. Next to the hangars was the military base; the hive of the Puritanists' army. Joshua pondered what had occurred earlier with mixed feelings. In a way, he'd accomplished an important part of the mission he'd been given, on the other hand, he'd lost a good chance at speeding the extermination process up. It didn't matter, he knew what Ethan's aims were. He hopped out of the cockpit and handed his helmet to a nearby trooper. Rubbing his beard, he exited the hangar and went straight for the tunnel that led into Procerus. After walking a short distance down the well-lit stone slab tunnel, he reached the end. He placed his finger in the slot beside a screen that checked his identity. After he was cleared the door opened to an elevator. Stepping inside, he again placed his finger in a slot that read fingerprints. Identifying him, he was cleared to take the elevator to the penthouse level.

Walking out into the penthouse suite, he was always surprised at how simple a man Ethan was. Ethan was happy to stay here most of the time, gazing down at the virgin forest below, sometimes going there for walks. He ate simple vegetables for each meal and occasionally drank organic wine. From up here, in his glass tower, Ethan could put his fingers into the world. He didn't need to take a step out. Turning, Ethan smiled broadly as Joshua walked in.

"I take it, he was there then," Ethan said bluntly.

"Yes, sir. I hadn't imagined that he would have been able to do it, but he seems to have accomplished consciousness transferal," said Joshua.

"What about Alyssa?" asked Ethan, not particularly concerned.

"Possibly destroyed, I didn't get to see the end of her battle with Ronald."

"I take it they've stopped the program. We've already received reports that the worker droids on the colonies are functioning normally and haven't been issued any new commands. Only Ronald could have accomplished it, his prints on the android would be sufficient to stop the program. But…it's fine. We've established that he successfully accomplished the transferal, so we can move on to the next step of our plan," said Ethan.

"But how will we get Ronald?" asked Joshua, a bit urgently. "The Front has been elusive to say the least and even up till now our attempts to find their hideout have all failed.

They've got a really tight cover going on their base of operations."

"That's not something we need to concern ourselves with Joshua," Ethan said knowingly. "He will come to us." Ethan removed a large key from his pocket. It had the Fact-ion's old emblem on it. Ethan fumbled the key absent mindedly. "Yes, he'll come to us soon."

Drew swooped down with a small squadron of unmanned armored flight suits following him. Raq was at the rear, remotely controlling flight suits. The fighting on the ground was sparse, occasional flashes of laser fire indicated that their ground force had been almost completely overrun. Approaching them, Raq could see the uniforms of the Puritanists and set her small squadron to lock on those targets. Trying to get them to only wound the soldiers was impossible so she could only hope for the best. As they reached the tops of the trees, Drew let loose a curtain of fire, felling Puritanist troops one after another. Raq sensed his anger.

Raq also felt a sense of urgency, but she had nothing against these men and women that fought blindly for a cause they probably thought was right. Releasing missiles, the unmanned flight suits shelled the area. Explosions ripped through the ranks of enemy troopers. Coming down to the forest floor, she dodged trees that came at her like giants. Breaking into a clearing where a platoon of Puritanists was gathered, she withdrew her katana and came to her feet, rushing them. They opened fire, but her self-learning system already knew how to cope with regular blaster shots. Ducking, bending, twisting, she plunged into their midst, slicing arms and legs. She plunged her katana's hilt into bellies, heads, knees and legs swept soldiers off their feet, bringing them down with lightning speed. Looking back at the group, they lay on the floor, bleeding, moaning and some even crying. No one dead. Good.

Drew fired indiscriminately into the crowd of enemies he saw before him. He couldn't count how many had dropped, how many were wailing, how much blood was sprayed over his armor. A shot hit him on the shoulder, taking an armor plate with it and singeing his skin. He didn't care, he continued to fire, screaming out the rage that ate away at him. He saw Zach lying nearby, his body motionless, his eyes wide open, staring. His blaster had lost all power. Drawing his katana, he roared as he charged towards the remaining troops. To his surprise, they all turned around and began to flee. He struck down one soldier from behind before he could make a getaway. What was going on? A hand came down on his shoulder.

"Drew," it was Raq's voice, "They're retreating. You can stop."

Drew looked down at his hands, shaking, caked in blood. He sheathed his sword and went over to Zach's body. Leaning over him, he closed Zach's eyes and said something to him that Raq couldn't hear. She guessed they used to be pretty tight. Turning to face Raq, Drew gazed into her eyes. She saw something was different about him.

"Why'd they retreat? They still outnumbered us," Drew said shakily.

"I'm not sure. They may have something else planned that we don't know about yet. I've got to get back to Chiyo up there. Can you take care of things down here?" Raq asked.

Drew stared at the carnage about him. "Yeah, I'll call in the medical team."

Raq arrived back up on the roof of Atanyal and went quickly down to see how Chiyo was doing. Chiyo sat hunched over the terminal, continually flicking through screens and typing. As Raq entered she looked up and smiled. Again, Raq had feelings she thought were probably inappropriate for a girl...even though she was a guy...ahh forget it.

"I can't shut it down Raq, look," Chiyo sighed. "I've tried to get into the system and get the androids in the colonies to gradually draw the inhabitants out of their comas and disconnect them from Elysium. I've devised a plan that they could use to do it slowly, so Elysium users won't have any serious withdrawals. They'll keep their Life Feeds for a while till we can get supplies to the various areas. The problem I have though is this..."

Raq gazed at the screen. 'Master Key Required' flashed in bright green letters. The master key. Raq had regained quite a few of her memories and an image of a master key flashed up in her mind. It had an FC for Fact-ion carved into it and came to a point that could be inserted into a terminal. Of course! She remembered now. It had been created so that no one could tamper with the essential functions of Elysium. Before any major changes could be made to the mainframe, the master key had to be inserted. More memories came flooding back to her, memories of a man, curly black hair, a well-trimmed black beard and mustache. He was laughing, smiling with...him. They were memories from before, when he'd been Ronald Kingsley. He'd been friends with this man, what was his name? Ethan, yes. Chiyo had mentioned him - the leader of the Puritanists. He had always kept the master key. That wasn't all, more memories were surfacing within her. Raq clutched her head as the memories of three lifetimes engulfed her.

Phase Thirteen

Illusion

Two weeks had passed since then. Chaya ordered that a large amount of troops be moved to Atanyal, due to the host controller being there. Chaya remained at the old base, but put Drew in charge of the forces at Atanyal, consisting of a few hundred men. Chaya had also told Raq and Chiyo to get to work on finding a way to shutdown Elysium. Chaya's intel had informed him that the Puritanists were on the move again, and this time, they were personally going to the colonies. He was worried that they would manually carry out extermination in the colonies one by one.

"Damnit!" shouted Raq, punching her hand down. "I just can't get in. All primary functions are impossible without the master key!"

Chiyo was anxious too. They weren't making any progress. "What about the memory wash function, were we able to take it down?" she asked.

"Yeah, people can jack in and out of Elysium without losing their memories now, but the problem is, everyone is already hooked in!" Raq said, exasperated.

"Is it possible for them to wake up from within Elysium? If they could, then there'd be no need for the master key. They could just pull their consciousnesses out and back into their bodies," Chiyo explained.

"To do that someone would have to...go in. Of course! I can go in. I transferred my consciousness out from the main frame before, there's no reason why I couldn't do it again. I can download my consciousness in. It's worth a shot!" while saying all this Raq was continually thinking of Xin Yu. Had she survived all of this? Would she be able to make it out? She didn't know but she had to give it a try.

"Alright," said Chiyo, "But you'll need to be able to connect to it somehow." Raq raised her finger.

"Just print identification? How's that possible?" Chiyo gasped.

"I'm not sure yet either, Chiyo. But something tells me I'll know soon enough." Raq walked over to the main terminal. "You'll need to maintain a connection with me through a link on that side, that way I'll be able to show the people over there that the whole of Elysium is just an illusion."

"Yeah," Chiyo said, "That way you'll be able to do just about anything over there. Whatever command you input, I'll just program it into the system and it will seem like it's really happening over there."

"Another thing, Chiyo. Keep my body connected to this terminal, in case I need to transfer out," Raq smiled at her.

Chiyo blushed a bit and turned away, "Don't do anything stupid, okay?"

Raq smiled even wider, her finger entering the slot. "C'mon. This is me." She winked at her. Raq's body stiffened suddenly, as if hit by a powerful electric current, then grew slack, finger still inserted.

"She's in," thought Chiyo.

It's that feeling again, I'm in but I'm out. Freefalling through snow, upon endless snow...White, checkered with black...it's unraveling me, bending looping and twisting me. I'm zipped, information being reduced to its most basic form. Now, a door appears. It's not a real door, just a space in the static, a wall of darkness that leads to the other side. I step through and I'm extracted, opened and poured out in a new container.

My eyes open on a familiar sight - the mother computer at the mainframe in Elysium. Staring downwards I see my old body again, Rak's body. It's strange, these weeks that I've spent in a woman's body made me so accustomed to it, now being back in a man's body feels bizarre. It feels as though I don't have a gender any more. I used to have a gender and an identity, but now I've been a man and a woman without a real body. So the idea of gender doesn't mean as much to me anymore. I look around, sad thoughts of Trent intrude on my mind. I can't think about them now, I have to focus. I search the area, Chiyo will probably upload a link for me somewhere around. There, on that desk.

Rak walked over and picked up the link. It looked like the one Eddie and Oliver had used. Rak pocketed it and headed out into the huge dome room with all the computer towers, then on to the exit. Inserting his finger in a nearby slot, the door slid open and he was in the lodge. Then, he climbed in the transit tube. He stood motionless inside it for a while. Where should he go? What should he do first? How could he convince these people that their existence was an illusion? Anyway, he'd find Xin Yu first and explain to her, then think of a plan for the rest. He had to hurry as well; a sense of urgency was eating away at him.

Chiyo stretched her arms. She'd been working for hours and she'd finally finished. The android Alyssa sat in a metal chair in front of her. Alyssa's arms and legs were shackled with thick metal bands, just in case she decided to go crazy. Chiyo had tweaked her programming though, so her android brain wouldn't only be thinking of her allegiance to the Puritanists.

"Oh, well. Let's give you a try," said Chiyo flipping the switch to a power feed that was connected to Alyssa's breast area. Alyssa's eyes lit up. Chiyo watched as she flexed all of her android muscles one by one, and then loosened them. Her face was relatively calm. "This should be easy enough," Chiyo thought. "Alyssa...Alyssa...how are your hearing and sight functions?"

"They are operating normally," came Alyssa's slightly raspy voice. Her head turned from side to side and then around

360 degrees. It was quite a normal thing for androids but Chiyo still couldn't help shuddering every time she saw it. Alyssa's gaze stopped on Chiyo, studying her. It made Chiyo feel as though she was being scanned.

"You look worried," said Alyssa finally.

"This android is definitely unique," Chiyo pondered, "Normal androids are unable to tell human emotion unless there are major face changes, but she can even tell I'm worried by a faint look in my eyes." Chiyo coughed, clearing her throat, "Is your memory of what has happened recently still intact?"

"Everything up to the moment I was knocked unconscious by that other android. Though knocked 'unconscious' wouldn't be a correct term…"

"Yes, I know. I fixed you up. I need some information from you, and depending on what happens after that we may…"

"How is Joshua?" asked Alyssa. Chiyo could even hear the concern in her voice. She'd removed any commands that had been programmed into her regarding the Puritanists, but Alyssa still felt a normal sense of concern for someone else.

"He's alive, I know that," Chiyo said abruptly. Alyssa's eyes almost looked sad, like she missed him. This was freaking Chiyo out too much, she'd never seen an android other than Raq display such emotion. How was this possible?

"A..Anyway, we need certain information from you regarding the location of the Puritanists' headquarters. You were situated there before, correct?" questioned Chiyo.

Alyssa's eyes lit up and a smile appeared, "Of course silly," she said playfully. "I spent most of my short life there." Chiyo was starting to feel that she couldn't treat her as an android anymore, though looking at her form it was so obvious she was. Her body wasn't as perfect as Raq's. The only thing that gave away Raq's body was the eyes. But Alyssa had quite a few features that were typical for an android.

"Fine, then...where is it located?" Chiyo tried assuming an interrogatory tone.

"You're going to find him right? The man in the glass tower?" Alyssa queried softly.

"The man in the glass tower?"

"That's what everyone calls him. Whenever I talked to the soldiers or other personnel, that's the name they use for him 'cause he's always up in that glass tower on the top. I wonder how everyone there is...I've got some good friends there y'know. I hope you don't want to hurt anyone," Alyssa said plainly.

"No, we don't want to hurt anyone. We just want to know where it is," said Chiyo, wondering if she was going to resist.

"That's fine, I'll tell you then..." said Alyssa, beaming. Chiyo's eyes widened even more. Was this girl...android...for real?

Rak had searched all the domes he thought Xin Yu would possibly be in, but he hadn't seen her.

"I hope she hasn't been exterminated..." Rak thought nervously. He made his way to the Residence Dome and looked her up. He found her dormitory and quickly transited there. Emerging in the lodge of her dormitory, he looked for her number. There it was. Waving his hand over a scanner screen at her door, he heard an electronic ring from the inside. Sounds of slow movement drew closer. The door slid open and Rak gazed at Xin Yu's deep blue eyes, the eyes he'd wanted to see for so long. Words suddenly fell away from him, useless objects that couldn't help him in this situation. She too stood in the doorway, staring straight into his eyes, wondering if she was dreaming. After a short pause, Xin Yu let go of her grip on the door and fell into Rak's arms.

"It's an illusion," thought Rak. "Her scent, her silky black hair, the warmth of her body...it's all not real. The small up and down movements she makes as she breathes, the feeling that I could stay like this forever with her head against my chest...it's all an illusion. But what a wonderful illusion." No, one thing wasn't an illusion, no matter which body he wore, this emotion within him wouldn't change...his love for this girl.

Rak used his link to create fantastic images and objects out of thin air and then made them vanish again. He did it to show Xin Yu what Elysium really was. He also told her the story of the world's recent history that he'd heard from Janu. He told her everything up to their most recent battle and his return to Elysium. It felt like they'd been talking the whole day when Rak finished his explanation and watched as Xin Yu's expression become confused.

"But Rak, you say that if a person's body is destroyed, their heart will stop beating and they'll die too, right? So, maybe your body isn't dead?"

"No, I'm pretty sure it is. I went through all the symptoms that those you've seen who die whilst still connected to Elysium have. But for some reason I didn't disappear. I know it has something to do with the person I was before, Ronald. He wasn't just researching cybernetics and technology. He was researching consciousness and its relationship to technology. Some of the details have come back to me, but some are still a blur. Anyway, what's important to know is that everyone here is just an icon, Xin Yu. An icon is a representation of someone who's lost their original memory. They need to be told this. If people wake up to this fact in large groups and start doing something about it, they may find a way out. As for me, I have to find Ethan, the guy who started all this with me some time ago, and get the master key back from him before he takes more lives here in Elysium," Rak said, a hint of desperation in his voice. Xin Yu clutched his hand and looked at him closely.

"Rak, I've got a feeling that this person, Ethan, doesn't want to kill off all the people in Elysium. If you think about it, he had control over the host controller for so long, he could have made his move to poison the people in Elysium long ago if he'd wanted to. Even now, he's waiting for something...and I think it's you Rak. Think about it, why did the troops at Atanyal that you told me about retreat when they still outnumbered you? And that guy Joshua, it sounds like he gave up on the host controller a little too easily. It's all too fishy."

Rak slumped back. Now that he thought about it, it did all seem odd. What were Ethan's real intentions? It's true, he could have wiped out Elysium ages ago, why didn't he do it then? Rak saw his link flashing, he touched it and a small screen popped up with Chiyo's face on it.

"So, have you found your girlfriend yet Raq?" Chiyo said loudly. Rak turned away from Xin Yu with an embarrassed look.

"I'm busy talking right now, is there something urgent?" snapped Rak.

"If you go out into Elysium, you'll probably see. Ethan has started to move on his own. He's sent some of his troopers to the colonies and is wiping out people jacked into Elysium randomly," Chiyo said.

"Damn!" yelled Rak. "This is his plot! He's trying to lure me to him, and he knows that killing people off is going to get to me."

"Okay Chiyo, I'll have to return there soon. Have you questioned Alyssa?"

"Yeah, she was surprisingly...cooperative."

"That's good...I guess. Anyway, I'll leave Xin Yu to try and spread the word to the people here. Get ready to transfer me."

"You got it," Chiyo's voice faded out.

"Xin Yu, do you think you can do this for me? These people need to be aware. If I do succeed then they'll need to be woken up and the process will be easier this way. Maybe, you can even find a way to wake up by yourselves...but without the master key, I just don't know..." Rak's voice trailed off.

Xin Yu gripped his hands tightly again, "I'll do it Rak."

Rak smiled, "Thanks Xin Yu. You know, I feel less and less human every day. Even more so here. When I realize that here and I'm just a floating piece of data, it kind of scares me. It feels like I'm disappearing..."

Xin Yu pinched his hand, faking a pouty face, "I disagree Rak. Even though you think you're disappearing, I think you're actually becoming more whole."

Rak's face changed and a determined look took over, "Okay, let's go."

Walking out into the dormitory halls, they could see it happening already. People were crowding around, watching in horror as another person became lifeless, flapping their arms around inanely and muttering mad things. When they emerged into the lodge it was the same. Yet another man, eyes rolled back, continually hitting his head into the wall of the lodge. Rak knew those people were gone. Exterminated. Their bodies were dead but an afterimage of their life, an icon, was still here.

Rak and Xin Yu kissed, as he entered the transit tube and headed back to the mainframe. He left his link with Xin Yu so she could use it to show the people here that everything was an illusion. In a short time he was back at the mother computer. Inserting his finger into the slot, he once again began to transfer himself into that other place called the 'real world.' He placed his hand over his heart. Even without a body, in Elysium or out of it, this heart of his was the only thing that was real. It wasn't an illusion.

Phase Fourteen

Flight

Drew. He'd always been a rational man. He'd handled battles in a level headed, tactical way and never allowed things to affect him personally, no matter how bad the situation got. He liked to think of himself as very logical and he lived his life just like it was a battle plan. It had its logical steps and order, its sequence of events. But logic had left him that day. Reason had left him that day. The day Zach died. He thought back on the days when they were in military school together. The great time they'd had. Zach had always been more rational than him. Whenever he wanted to climb out of the base to go out, or steal a flight suit to go for a joy ride, Zach had always been the one to bring him back down to earth. Back down to earth. He was down on the earth now, and the weight of it was crushing him. When they'd graduated from military school and joined the Fact-ion they were full of bright hopes for the future. People in the streets would hold their hands and greet them like heroes. Hell, they were heroes. They'd done what other people never dared to. They stood up to the ancient powers that had ruled the earth and raped it for such a long time. Even after the split, it was Zach who was objective enough to be able to see which side was the right one to take. Drew's loyalty had always been with the military, but people had to fight for a purpose, not just an organization. Zach had seen the purpose behind the Fact-ion clearly and he knew that the Front was the right way to go. What was the right way to go now? The firm pillar that he'd had was gone, and Drew faltered with each step he took.

His hands were clammy as he gripped the joystick of the aircraft he'd commandeered from the hangars. He'd received no authority, no orders from Chaya. This was his own vendetta. He knew that what he was doing wasn't going to help much, but he didn't care. He was falling down, and he wanted to take them along with him.

Raq. Staring at the android seated in front of her, she had this weird sense of déjà vu. How did she know this...person? Alyssa was so like a person, and herself being in an android body, she could relate to her completely. They'd released her from the shackles and she sat happily on the chair, flipping through screens at a nearby terminal and playing games. How had she achieved consciousness? What had happened to her?

Chiyo's voice broke through her cloud of thought, "Raq, Drew's done something stupid."

Raq peered up at her face, sensing tension, "What's he gone and done?"

"He's stolen a plane and is heading for Procerus. On his own."

It came back to Raq now. That look in Drew's eyes, how it had changed during the battle at Atanyal. It wasn't that it had changed, it was more like the light had gone out.

Chiyo said, "I think I know why. He kind of lost it after Zach died. He was acting really strange. His hands were shaking. I saw him polishing his laser gun over and over again. Something snapped in him. Now he's gone off on some suicidal revenge mission."

Raq stared off into space. Even though it wasn't a good thing, it kind of fell in sync with Raq's own plans. She knew she had to confront Ethan. Chaya would never let her do it alone. Chaya'd insist on a full attack, which despite everything would be a hopeless fight. This was perfect really.

"I'm going Chiyo," Raq said. "I've got to face him personally. For some reason he wants me. I've got to find out why. He's killing people off in Elysium as though they're pawns in his mad game. I just can't let that go. I'm going to meet him.

Somehow, I know he'll let me get close to him. Then I can finally solve this whole mystery and hopefully put an end to this."

"I kind of knew you were going to say that. I've got three flight suits already in the hangar," Chiyo smirked.

Raq opened her mouth to argue, then saw Chiyo's face and knew she'd never be able to convince her. "You said...three?"

Chiyo slapped Alyssa on the back and she stared up at Chiyo, "I figured she'd come in handy, and she's not doing anything useful around here anyway...just playing games every day."

It was true, Alyssa's knowledge of Procerus and its location would be invaluable. Raq didn't bother debating, but just watched the two. "What an unlikely trio," he thought. "Or perhaps...it's just right."

"We need to move...fast," said Raq.

Joshua. Walking through the large barracks beside Procerus, soldiers saluted him as he passed. Joshua rubbed his beard as he contemplated Ethan's plan. Ever since he'd heard it, it had become the focus of his life, his reason for living. He saw himself as a key figure in the evolution of humanity, moving people onto the next stage of the ladder. A beautiful ladder that ascended higher and higher. He'd seen the way that life evolved in the forest that lay in front of Procerus. It changed and adapted to circumstances. Just like in the past. All forms of life evolved in order to cope with their environments. Creatures from the sea had come to land and developed lungs. Reptiles had grown wings and taken to the skies. Apes had come down from the trees and stood on two feet. Their brains evolved to meet with the new world they faced. The earth was no longer in danger of extinction. Now, people could take the next step and leave the cradle. He was looking forward to it.

Raq and Chiyo, clothed in armored flight suits, followed Alyssa as she darted through the air. Flight suits couldn't achieve high altitudes like airplanes, but they were still about a hundred meters in the air. Below them the emerald green canopies of regenerated forests spread out, blanketing the ground. Occasionally, lakes spilled out amidst the foliage, turquoise waters shining under the sun's countenance. Alyssa flew really fast, Raq had no problem keeping up as her body was already adjusting to Alyssa's flight patterns and speed but she lagged behind deliberately for Chiyo.

"Geez, is she a speed freak or what? Tell her to slow down Raq! I'm scared of heights, you know!" Chiyo groaned.

"At this speed, we should be able to make it in time," Raq replied, winking at Chiyo.

She stuck out her tongue at Raq, then immediately pulled it back in, the icy air nearly freezing it up.

Raq admired the scenery. This was the first time she'd been able to have a good look at the regenerated forests. They were a real sight to behold. Life was allowed to carry on inside the forests, without people interfering. It was a perfect world. Why then, did Ethan have to try and destroy this peace that was bought at such a cost? Raq felt anger burning within her. Why did he want to waste the blood, sweat and tears of millions? And just kill off others, as if they were nothing? Raq hadn't felt this kind of strong rage in a long time. She blazed her trail toward Procerus, with just one thought in her mind, "I'm going to put an end to Ethan..."

Bringing the aircraft down from the clouds, Drew came into view of Procerus. It was quite an awesome sight...he might have thought before. He didn't care for that anymore. He checked his armory, he was fully loaded with missiles, lasers and explosive tipped bullets. The glass tower came closer into view, closer and closer. He could start to...a red light flickered on his screen, flight suits incoming. They weren't going to make it easy for him. Well, that was just fine. Bringing the plane down lower he locked on to the approaching suits and let loose a volley of missiles. Streaking towards their targets, the missiles were like worms, leaving a silk trail in the air. Some missiles connected, turning the enemy suits into cocoons of fire. Others evaded and rose towards him. Drew turned his laser cannon towards them, releasing streaks of red death into the blue air. Some suits were caught by the fire, veering off, smoke pouring from their shells. The one's that dodged came into Drew's range.

"Now!" he thought. He spun his plane around, like a top in the air, an insane dancer spitting bullets from his iron heart. The bullets lit up the air, fireflies fluttering at anything that lived, seeking their light. More suits blew up, flames embracing them. One made it through his barrage. Getting near, he shot at Drew.

"Too slow!" screamed Drew, the excitement of the dogfight intoxicating him. Drunk on the energy of conflict, he dove down before the flight suit could get a clear shot. He released another missile as he went down, hitting the intruder squarely in the chest. Beneath his bird's metal talons, he saw more flight suits, like insects below. Again, he released round after round of laser fire and bullets into their midst. The insects scattered, some caught by his fiery bursts, others narrowly eluding them. But they were in close now. He'd lost the advantage of distance that aircraft had over flight suits. Surrounded by bugs, he let all his artillery go. Missiles erupted from his metal exoskeleton, lasers flicked out their red tongues and bullets dispersed. Flight suits around him plummeted, hitting others on their way down, dragging unwilling victims. Explosions bloomed and crackled, as the air itself caught fire. He didn't even see it coming, a clean straight shot from one flight suits. It tore through his thick metal covering in one go, slicing his armored bird through its center. He hung in the air for a moment, and then tumbled from the sky. Drew tried everything he knew to bring the plane upright and resume flight, but the main engines had been destroyed. The panorama of the virgin forest near Procerus spun in his vision as he sped to meet the ground.

Alyssa emerged from a bank of mist and the towering image of Procerus came into view. Raq followed closely behind, holding a very giddy-looking Chiyo's hand. Flying low, with cloaking devices set to maximum, their chances of being spotted in flight suits was minimal. Alyssa glided above the emerald crown of the trees, the ominous glass giant looming closer. Above them, a battle was taking place in the heavens. Laser fire sparkled and gunshots rang out. Explosions peppered the sky in a deadly array and Raq saw a lone plane dropping. It had to be...Drew! Raq fired the fuel injection booster in her pack and immediately shot out ahead of Alyssa, her eyes continually on the falling machine. Raq caught up with it and quickly ripped the windshield off the cockpit, snapped Drew's safety belt and pulled him out. He was unconscious. The plane struck the ground at a high speed, sending shards of metal launching off in all directions. It blew up a second later, as Raq touched down on the forest's moist earth bed. She signaled for the others to hide, and they all did. A few Puritanist flight suits came to check the wreckage and left shortly after.

Drew began to come around a few minutes later. His head had been cut, and Chiyo had wrapped some cloth around it, otherwise he had no serious injuries. He sat up abruptly.

"The plane! I've gotta get the plane! The Puritanists, I'm gonna beat them, I..." looking around he remembered what had happened. Tears started to well up in his eyes. He covered them with his arm and punched at the ground, over and over.

"Shit! Shit! Shiiiittt! I'm so useless, I couldn't do anything! I'm so pathetic I might as well die right here!" Drew spat out. Chiyo slapped Drew across the face. Hard. He looked up at her in amazement as if he'd suddenly woken up from a dream.

"Get a grip Drew! You just pulled a crazy stunt and nearly threw your life away. Don't you think there are people who care about you? You...idiot!" Chiyo turned away from him. "And don't go saying stuff like 'I might as well die right here!' Look around dickhead. We've all lost something, not just you. I lost my family, Raq lost her friggin' body and Alyssa didn't even have a life to begin with. What you complainin' about? We're all trying Drew, trying our best to unravel this mess up that's been created. But it's not going to be solved by going ballistic."

Drew stared at the people with him. She was right, he'd really lost it these past few weeks. This wasn't what Zach would have done. He'd have made a plan and started to act. Standing up, he wiped his tears.

"You're right. I've been a complete prick. Forgive me okay?"

Chiyo stood up, "Sheesh, it's about time. What next boss?" Chiyo turned over to Raq.

"Well, I think trying to get some uniforms and sneak in sounds like a good option, and we can use Alyssa's knowledge of the place to try and locate where Ethan is as soon as possible," Raq answered. "Alyssa, how different do you look from the other androids?"

"My model was a common one so there are many worker droids that look similar to me," replied Alyssa.

"Excellent," said Raq.

Phase Fifteen

Jam

"Do you really think this is going to work?" Chiyo tried whispering but it still came out loud. Raq looked around nervously as they pulled the bodies of three soldiers they'd just knocked unconscious into a nearby janitor's room. Raq raised a finger to her lips and Drew just rolled his eyes back. Typical Chiyo.

Each of them had one unconscious trooper, all males, on the floor of the janitor's room in front of them. Chiyo was sizing them up, searching for the right size. Raq immediately started stripping her clothes off, forgetting that Drew was also in the room.

Chiyo looked at Raq in shock, "Raq, I think us *girls* should change in that little room over there." Raq suddenly noticed that her cleavage was exposed and that Drew was staring intently. Her face turned hot and red as she tried to cover herself with her arm.

"Right, let's go…" she ran off into a smaller adjacent room. Chiyo and Alyssa followed. Soon they emerged, fully dressed in Puritanists' uniforms.

"Well, it's a good thing the women and men's uniforms are the same," Chiyo said, eyeing her jump suit critically. "I don't think this guy bathed often though," she said, wrinkling up her nose.

Drew was at the entrance, "Okay, the coast is clear." The four of them walked down a long corridor directly into the military barracks. Alyssa said that there was an entrance tunnel that led to Procerus at the end. Going down the large hallway, they tried to look as natural as possible. Raq had just gotten used to putting a bit of a sway into how she walked, so trying to walk stiffly was another challenge. In general, they looked suspicious. Fortunately, the soldiers they'd seen so far were usually on their own and weren't in large groups. As they were coming to the end of the hallway, they saw the large entrance door to the tunnel that obviously went to Procerus. Drew and Chiyo's faces perked up a bit, only to drop as a different group of soldiers marched out from a side corridor.

They wore purple berets, and they heard Alyssa whisper, "The Inspection Unit."

"Hell," cursed Drew, his hand reaching to the holster at his side. Raq put her hand on his shoulder, signaling him to wait. Trying to appear as normal as possible, they strutted past the Inspection Unit.

"They don't seem to have noticed anything," thought Raq, and they all continued to the tunnel entrance. They almost reached it when a shout from behind them made them freeze in their tracks.

"You there! Androids aren't permitted near the Procerus tunnel without permission. Let me see your passes!" A huge voice bellowed.

Drew was the first one to turn around and the rest followed him. Drew quickly assessed the situation, a squad of about ten troopers, each armed with laser rifles, possibly other weapons. There was no way; they'd have to chance it.

"Oh sure," Drew muttered, reaching to his side, "Our passes are right here..." Drawing his phaser, he aimed and fired a clear shot at the man who just spoke. Drew's blast penetrated him through the chest, and he immediately dropped to the floor, while the others stood around, stunned.

Raq reached for her phaser but felt Chiyo's hand touch hers. Shaking her head, she pointed her jaw in the direction of the tunnel. She tacitly understood what Chiyo meant. Whatever way they looked at it, they were bound to be caught eventually. Raq had to quickly find Ethan and end all of this.

"Go, Raq! We'll handle things here," Drew yelled.

Taking one last glimpse at them all, Raq ran off down the tunnel. The slabs on the walls were old and familiar, in a strange way. Had she been here before? Running on, she got to the end of the tunnel. Would this work? If the situation was the way she thought, she should be able to insert her finger in this slot...and the door would open. And it did. Again, inside the elevator, inserting her finger, she selected the top floor, which had off limits clearly written next to it. "Access granted..." popped up. Just as she thought again. The elevator rose quickly, and came to a sudden halt on the top floor. The doors slid open, and Raq emerged into a sparsely furnished penthouse suite. To her right was a long meeting table, and on her left a huge array of clear glass windows. In front of her stood a man she'd seen before. Joshua. He was dressed in combat armor, a kind he'd never seen. It had the appearance of regular armor, but had a vaster array of weapons. In one hand, he held a laser cannon, in the other, a long saber. His head armor was also fitted with two mini lasers. On his back, another long weapon that looked like a grenade launcher was holstered. Next to him was another man whom she'd never seen, but was even more familiar than the other. Ethan. Holding a glass of wine in his hand, he raised it to Raq in a mock toast.

"What took you so long Ronald? I was beginning to get impatient," Ethan said cynically. All Raq's muscles clenched at once.

Drew, Chiyo and Alyssa had taken cover behind the frames on either side of the tunnel that Raq had just entered. They'd taken down most of the men from the Inspection Unit, but they could already hear the shouts and hollers of backup on the way. Chiyo was again amazed at Alyssa's reaction to the situation. She was backing them up like a comrade, and her skills were excellent. In just a short time, had she become loyal to them? Or was there another reason? Another wave of troopers was approaching. Drew checked his phaser, it had fully charged again and he had a few grenades that he'd picked up from the soldiers they'd knocked out. Still, he didn't know how long they could hold out; soon the whole damn army was going to be here. Chiyo also readied her rifle as the soldiers approached, and then she saw something flit past her at an incredible speed. It was Alyssa. She stood right in the middle of the entrance, facing the oncoming forces with her saber in her hand, without any cover at all!

"What's the matter Ronald? It still hasn't come back to you yet?" asked Ethan, meandering off to the side and gazing at the forest below. Swirling his wine in his hand, he turned again to Raq, "Don't worry, you weren't supposed to remember. After all you weren't Ronald to begin with." Raq's confused expression made Ethan's smirk grow even bigger. "Oh, you've really got it. His expressions, his mannerisms, it's incredible. But you're still not him. You've been told that you were Ronald Alexander Kingsley…a convenient and necessary story. For many reasons, however, it's completely untrue. You see, I killed Ronald Kingsley with my own hands, so I'd be the one to know right?"

Alyssa wasn't fighting, she was dancing. Charging straight at the oncoming troops, she leapt into the air in front of them, and before hitting the floor, right in the middle of the group, she'd already taken down three of them with her blaster. Before the troopers could react, she raised her saber, flicking it from side to side in a macabre ribbon dance, she caught shoulders, legs and arms as she spun around, blood splattering her jump suit. Then she spun around with her saber at neck level, a deadly ballerina moving across the battle stage. Men groaned as their necks were cut. As she reached the side, one of the trooper's heads flew into the air, decapitated. At a distance now, the remaining men pulled out their blasters, just as Chiyo and Drew gave her supporting fire from the rear. Of the four men left, three were blasting at Alyssa and one was focused on Drew and Chiyo. Drew aimed for the soldier, and Chiyo focused on the other three. Alyssa took a hit in the side of her stomach, blasting away a small portion of her body, but her face showed no pain. She charged at the men once again. One of them fell as she rushed them, hit by Chiyo's shot. Alyssa leapt for the last two, spinning in the air to avoid their blasts. She skewered the first trooper, shielding herself with his body, while the other blasted shots at her. Chiyo took him down. Drew had to come out a little to get a clear shot, and the last trooper facing him started firing a rapid volley of shots. As Drew had aimed and let loose a laser, a blast seared into his leg, making him fall down on one knee. Peering up through the agony clouding his vision, he saw that his shot had struck his opponent down, before passing out.

"How's that? Sounds impossible right? Oh...he's lying! Is what you must be thinking. But I'm afraid not," Ethan continued. "Ronald...I'll call you that, even though you aren't really him. There are two big problems with humanity: ignorance and mortality. Ignorance is the biggest one. We've both seen the effects of ignorance. The world we were born into was one that had been nearly obliterated by war. Tales of animals living in fields and jungles were like fairy tales to us. That was the result of humanity's ignorance. Whether or not war was the best way to solve the problem was debatable, but that was the situation we found ourselves in. We were young when the reconstruction began. I have fond memories of those days Ronald. All of us working toward a common goal, to bring back the glory of nature! It felt for a while that we'd really achieved harmony. Fighting was a thing of the past, environmental abuse, animal abuse, even serious illnesses became a thing of the past. And looking around outside you can see what we've done. However, I saw cracks Ronald, cracks in that harmony...called ignorance."

"The ignorance of idealists like you once were. Believing that everyone had the right to this Utopia we'd toiled to create!"

Ethan threw his wine goblet at the glass pane. It shattered and its contents dripped down like blood. "You wanted to let everyone into the newly rebuilt areas, so that they could just pollute them again! You said that with time and patience they would come to understand how to care for the environment. You wanted to allow them free access to Elysium, to give them a place in the virtual realm that was the solution we'd created to people continually plundering the earth. If I had allowed all these things Ronald, what kind of world would we be living in now? The ignorance I'd seen in the dictators of the past, I started to see in you Ronald. That's when I started to make my plan."

Raq had already heard enough. Targeting Joshua weapons, she tried to locate their wireless signals…none. Why? It didn't matter. Raq drew her blaster from the holster at her side.

"I didn't come here to talk Ethan. I came here to…destroy you and your plans!" Raq started to fire, but Joshua immediately pounced at Raq. His armored suit had a deadly aura about it. It was fast, Raq couldn't evade his first blow and it sent her skidding back on the smooth floor. Quickly aiming, Raq blasted, but Joshua was gone. Above her, she heard the faint sound of something coming down. She barely had a second to move. Joshua's long blade sliced through her arm. Raq gazed in amazement at the severed limb that had been attached to her a second ago. How on earth? Scanning the area frantically, Raq wondered why the self-learning system wasn't keeping up with his movements. Another attack came from the side, again Raq had no idea where he was coming from. She felt herself fall, her right leg no longer holding her up. Falling face first to the concrete, she used her remaining arm to flip herself over. Where was he? If she could only locate him somehow…She decided to just blast away randomly, hoping a stray shot would hit her attacker. Then something flew over her, it was a blur in her vision, but it was definitely Joshua's suit. In disbelief, she watched her own arm clutching the blaster sail into the air above her, before clattering on the floor a few meters away. The arm bled a shiny metallic alloy. She felt no pain, her internal and external pain functions had been turned off. Clanking sounds of steel on concrete approached. Towering over her, she saw Joshua grin at her as he raised his blade, and took her remaining leg off in a spurt of silver. His metallic arms reached down, and picked up what was left of her. He carried her in his arms, into an adjacent room. While walking, she heard Ethan's droning.

"Sorry to be such a cheat, but I'm quite aware of the functions that body of yours has. After all, I watched you make it. First of all, Joshua's weapons are deliberately not fitted with wireless receivers. Also, as soon as you stepped into this room your self-learning functions were jammed by powerful transmitters. Otherwise, it might have been me and my dear comrade getting all chopped up...and we wouldn't want that, now would we?"

Joshua placed Raq into a long, stretcher style bed and fastened a firm strap across her chest. She was immobile. Around her, there were terminals and all manner of electronic equipment.

Ethan's face loomed over her, "Well now, shall I continue my story? I was just getting to the best part..."

Phase Sixteen

The Evolution of the Machine

Raq lay tethered to a stretcher in what appeared to be an operating room. There were intravenous drips in the corner, what seemed to be an operating table on her left side and a large computer encased in metal behind her. Wires and cables ran from the computer's metal casing to the operating table. On the table she could see that the wires and cables were connected to small suctions. It came back to her...it was called a brain machine interface (BMI). She had memories of Ronald using them before.

"Look familiar Ronald? This is the brain machine interface you used quite a lot. Anyway back to our discussion. My second problem with humanity is mortality. The fact that we live such short and meager existences is bothersome enough. What's worse is that the wisdom of the past can never be passed down properly by just relying on the 'next generation'." Ethan put his face so close to Raq's that she could smell the wine on his breath. "I don't trust the next generation Ronald. So, to make sure the world remains a paradise I need to continue my existence. But as we found out long ago, life is truly short and thus prolonging it beyond the average hundred years is nearly impossible. Of course, you weren't interested in living longer; you did your research in the hope of creating better lives for people or even saving those who were terminally ill by giving them a new body to place their consciousness in. Such grand ideals Ronald!"

"I believe you've already met Alyssa. She was one of our first successful test subjects. When you were the leader of cybernetics at the Fact-ion we were searching for a way to transfer human consciousness into androids. There were quite a few test subjects in the beginning but most of them went haywire after performing the BMI. There was something missing. That's when you started to become all mystical Ronald. You studied the spiritual techniques of the East and their methods of releasing the consciousness from the body. That, combined with the BMI, gave birth to Alyssa. Her consciousness came from that of a girl who had a rare disease and only a few months to live. You so kindly taught her breathing and meditation techniques daily until nearly the moment of her death. When she was about to pass away you performed the meditation and breathing combined with BMI. Her consciousness was successfully transferred to the data acquisition box and then to her new android body."

"When she first awakened, she was basically the same as an android and you nearly gave up hope until you saw her watering that plant in the lab one day. That was something no ordinary android would have done without programming. The only limiting thing was her body. It was an older, cruder body that only resembled a human's but on close observance was still mechanical. All fired up at your success you began work on this...your greatest creation Ronald...your current body. It completely resembled a human in every way and could even cut off some of the more troublesome human functions. What a masterpiece! If only you hadn't decided to side with those imbeciles Arthur Amano and Chaya, we might still be together now. But let's not dwell on the past shall we? What interests me is the present! I plan on deleting your presence from that body Ronald and installing my own consciousness in it. I know it's a bit beat up, but that's something that can be solved quickly..."

Alyssa watched Drew drop behind her. Chiyo was still okay, crouching behind the entrance pillars, but she was panting and exhausted. More men would definitely arrive soon. Alyssa's mind couldn't help going back to that time. The man with kind eyes had sat next to her every day, holding her hand, comforting her. She knew that she was going to die, yet somehow he made it all seem okay. As if death wouldn't be the end for her. Every day she'd practice breathing and let her consciousness leave her body. The man had told her never to get too far away from her body, or else she might not be able to come back. So she'd travel around the room, watching her weak body lying still on the bed, its chest rising and falling. Sometimes she'd leave the room, just to get a peek. And when she did, she'd never felt so free. It was beautiful outside the room. She'd seen it before, but seeing it through bodiless eyes was different. She saw more. The trees and forests were more than just green beauties stuck in the ground; they were shining pretty emerald things with sparkling sticks that ran down into a rich loam that just bustled with life. The sky was an endless blue playground for clouds that shifted and changed into unpredictable creatures. Why had she never seen all of this before? Then, a touch on her sleeping body pulled her consciousness back in. It was him, the man with the kind eyes.

"You shouldn't go for too long you know..." he said softly.

She nodded and smiled at him...what was his name again? Coming back to the present moment, she darted to pick up Chiyo and Drew, holding each in one arm.

"Hey!" Chiyo protested. "I can still fight. Put me down!" The shouts and yells of soldiers were getting closer. Alyssa dashed into an empty room; it looked like it was used for storage. She put Chiyo and Drew down on the floor and turned to leave. Chiyo was about to protest again.

"His wound needs attention," said Alyssa, walking out. Before disappearing, she said, "If you see Raq again tell him...her...I said thank you for everything. Keep out of sight."

"Oh, I remember now," Alyssa thought as a squad of about twenty men, this time in battle armor, came stomping at her. Tumbling to the side of the corridor, she tossed a grenade she'd picked out of Drew's suit. A laser blast struck her in the arm as it exploded, sending bodies spewing out of its fiery center. She switched her blaster to her good arm without waiting for the smoke to clear. She could see the infrared signatures of the soldiers clearly. Letting off carefully aimed shots, she took down three troopers before something seared through her leg. Looking down, circuits crackled and spat electricity where her calf had been. "His name was..." Shooting again, another two soldiers fell to her precise shots, before another blast went straight through her chest. Freezing, the blaster fell out of her unwillingly hands. Her chest sparked and the machinery within her exposed itself. As she swayed and closed her eyes she finally remembered. "Yes, it was Ronald."

Raq lost consciousness briefly. Drifting in a dreamlike state, memories of the past came back to her. She remembered arguing with Ethan and deciding to leave the Fact-ion. Taking his work with him, Ronald had snuck the new android body he'd been working on out of the Fact-ion's labs before Ethan could discover it. He entrusted the android that he'd finished to Chaya and went into hiding for a while. But the Puritanists moved quickly. Shortly after, they assassinated Arthur and his wife. Ethan came looking for him personally. He remembered jacking into Elysium, just as the door to his cubicle had broken down. The rest was a blur, it didn't make any sense. How could she have all of Ronald's memories? Ethan had said that she wasn't Ronald.

Her mind swam back up to the surface and she opened her eyes. Coming to, she searched the room for Ethan. He was lying on a stretcher next to her with BMI plugs attached to his head. Joshua finished attaching the last one, and stepped back.

Raq turned to gaze at Ethan and asked, "You said I wasn't Ronald. So why do I have all of his memories?"

"You can't be Ronald. I shot him in the back of the head while he was jacked into Elysium. He died on the spot, I made sure of it. He probably also did a BMI before his death and transferred his memories to a hard drive. Then, I assume they loaded them into you when you transferred out of Elysium," Ethan said with a disinterested tone.

Raq knew it wasn't true. She'd started to have flashbacks of Ronald's memories while she was still in Elysium, and no one had downloaded any other memories into her. Ethan was definitely wrong!

"And what do you plan on doing…now?" she asked hesitantly.

"You do ask some annoying questions. Very well, I'll tell you. These plugs attached to my head will extract my consciousness from my body at the very moment Joshua plunges those…" he gestured to two blades with cables attached, "Into my body and yours. The resulting effect will be to erase your consciousness from that body and implant mine. At the same moment, I will be hooked up to the data acquisition box which I've networked to Elysium. You see, I don't just plan to overcome *my* mortality problem. In order to make sure ignorance never overruns this planet of ours again I'm going to jack into Elysium. One thing you never had a chance to realize is that this body *is* the master key to Elysium. It has the capacity to open any dome in Elysium, I'm sure you noticed that, right? At the same time it can also connect to any user that's jacked in to Elysium and issue commands to them. Effectively once I'm in, I'll be able to alter the memories of everyone who's jacked in to Elysium and turn them into my servants. I can make their objectives mine, and set them on fulfilling my purpose, which is to take control of the remaining measly governments on this planet with an army of obedient brainwashed slaves! It's perfect, don't you think? And I have to hand it to you Ronald, or whatever is left of Ronald in you. I truly couldn't have done it without you."

Ethan closed his eyes and said to Joshua, "You may begin now."

Phase Seventeen

Beyond

"Hello, welcome to Elysium. The answer to all your business and entertainment needs. Please state you name and I.D number and then we can get started."

A brief pause.

"Thank you Ronald Alexander Kingsley. You are now ready to create your profile! First make an icon of yourself. This icon will be the body that you will use in Elysium to perform all your daily tasks. Please select your face shape, body, skin color, hair color, hair style, apparel and any accessories that you want."

Silence again.

"Now please enter an alias that you will be using in Elysium, real names are allowed, but are to be used at your own risk. Now complete the information form you see on the screen with the details of which company you will be working for. Any credits you have may be transferred from your bank account to your own personal one here in Elysium. "

"Thank you, Rak. You are now ready to enter the world of Elysium. Please have a look at our Dormitories and choose a room you like to be your base of operations."

Yes, I remember the first time I logged into Elysium and created this imaginary being. I went back a few times and found work with Mr. Lin's company. I enjoyed playing fighter kites in room Y23 and I met Yui. Yui, I miss her so much...

"Pleased to meet you Miss, uhhh..."

"Just Yui will do fine. You could add Miss onto that but I wouldn't want to give you too many things to remember," Yui said.

"I don't have a problem remembering things; I just have a problem using the correct words. If I just called you Yui, you could misinterpret my intentions and think I was being overly affectionate. At the same time, calling you Miss Yui makes me feel like I'm being too respectful and distant, don't you think?" Rak shot back.

"I see you have difficulty making decisions quickly..." Yui responded.

"Alright, alright...Yui," Rak looked at her through one open eye. "Miss Yui," he finished.

No wait...before then, I need to go even further back. The door broke down, I was jacked into Elysium. I could literally feel the laser about to burn through my skull. And...I jumped. That's it, I jumped. Just like I'd done before when meditating, my consciousness left my body. But instead of floating around the room, it went straight into Elysium and Rak. I lost my memories of what had happened before...the memories of my whole life. Ethan must have done something to the host controller. Everyone in Elysium was the same. They went about their daily existences, but they forgot their bodies were outside and jacked into a machine.

I did it again. I jumped again.

Joshua stabbed the wired blade into Ethan's heart. He didn't scream in pain. Blood fountained from the wound, but Ethan didn't even move a muscle. His consciousness was ready to leap into Raq's body. Raq knew what to do, it came back to her. Just like she'd done back then - she jumped out. Peering down, she floated above her mutilated body and watched as Joshua stabbed the wired blade into a port in her chest. Formless, she moved in closer, staring into the eyes of her old body. Suddenly, they lit up and Joshua leaned in closer.

"Ethan, sir. Is that you?" Joshua spoke in a trembling voice. Silence stuffed the air as minutes passed. Raq could feel something pulling at her. It was pulling her up, into that all penetrating light that she'd seen before when her consciousness left her body. She knew she'd never come back if she went there now. Looking around she saw the data acquisition box. She was bodiless, pure consciousness, not jacked in to any connection, how could she possibly get in? It didn't matter; she still had to give it a try. Resisting the pull towards the light she forced herself into the acquisition box. It was her last chance, she knew it.

"Jo...sh..ua. Be..gin...trans...ferring...me to the...data acquisition...box, then I will...enter the network and Elysium," Ethan said. Joshua removed the wired blade from Ethan's now dead corpse and plunged it into the data acquisition box. A screen appeared before him and he started flipping through menus. Eventually he came to the option 'Begin Transfer.' Joshua selected it. Ethan's eyes widened briefly, and then went dark. 'Transfer Complete', popped up on the screen and Joshua grinned.

Raq found herself in a long hallway. On both sides of her, huge white walls reached up. The walls reached about fifty meters into the air and beyond them was a ceiling that seemed to be made of one solid sheet of steel. Peering closer at the walls she saw that they were filled with screens. Each screen had the face and information of every icon in Elysium. They were all moving around on the screens, each absorbed in their daily activities. Interestingly, they were all alone. They were all doing something, but there was no one and nothing around them. They were like puppets performing without an audience and lacking a stage.

It was true, Raq mused. Elysium created the perfect illusion that one was interacting with others, hearing sounds, touching, smelling and feeling, however in reality, they were just alone. Raq realized that this was Elysium's data bank. Moving further down the hallway, the surroundings began to change. The walls became a dark green and thick white lines ran like tracks down them, going straight ahead. Electronic components jutted out from the white tracks at different points along the walls. This had to be Elysium's CPU. Plodding further down, she could see all the tracks led to a hub on a wall at the end of the hallway. The hub had a screen that glowed an ultra violet hue and it flickered slowly as though it was a beating heart. Someone stood in front of it. The person had long tangled orange hair. He wore a white suit with matching pants and black shiny shoes. As he turned, Raq saw that his face was completely white, like a mime, and his eyes were an insane red. His cheek had a purple FC imprinted on it. Just like the master key. It was the Fact-ion's old logo.

"Ethan," breathed Raq.

Ethan stared at him, eyes darting around before he chuckled and said, "Ronald, my dear boy! You never cease to amaze me! For you to be here means you're either a figment of my imagination, or you truly learnt how to transfer your consciousness without the need for any interface…any connection. Truly incredible! Not that it matters, I control your old body, the master key to Elysium. And here we are Ronald! The CPU! The brain of that world. Whatever I input here will become reality for the users of Elysium! Can you imagine it Ronald? There are possibly more than a million users of Elysium worldwide. By altering their memories I can make them become my willing slaves. Once I have completely annihilated all opposition, I'll return and fix up that old body of yours to enjoy my immortality in the world that I've always wanted. Isn't it splendid Ronald? Isn't it worth rejoicing for?"

Raq clenched her fist. Through gritted teeth she said, "Do you really believe I'd let you do that you manic? It's over for you Ethan! Right…NOW!!"

Raq charged at him, creating a silver blue saber in her hand. As she reached him, she plunged it into his stomach. To her amazement, he didn't even react. The saber just went through him, as though it wasn't real at all.

"Oh Ronald you're still so dramatic! You forget that your old android body is mine now. All its pain and sensory functions are off. In this place, I'm just like you...pure consciousness. What harm could we do to one another? It would be better for you to just step back and watch Ronald, as I usher in a new era!" Ethan chuckled again.

Raq jabbed again and again at Ethan in frustration as he started to connect with all the Icons in Elysium through the hub. "I can feel their minds Ronald," Ethan smirked. "Their sleeping, unaware minds. Such futile existences, don't you think? Living in cyberspace and never really accomplishing anything...I'll change all that! I'll give them a sublime purpose!"

Raq saw a menu with 'Execute' appear on the hub's screen and grew frantic. Ethan hit it, and it faded. Raq was thinking and thinking, "What? What? What...can I do!!??" Ethan's face grew wider in expectation, and then...

'Access Denied' flashed on the screen. "Whaaaaattt?" screamed Ethan. Pressing 'execute' again and again. Raq relaxed a little.

"Access denied...but why? He's using my body, the master key; it should allow him access to all Elysium's CPU functions," Raq thought. Ethan was hitting and kicking at the terminal, all to no effect. It wouldn't grant him access. He started to laugh; it was a bitter, hopeless kind of laugh as he realized his plan had been destroyed.

"Of course," he said, his hands shaking, "I'll just transfer out of here. Go back to my body and start again! Yes! I'll..."

Raq placed her hands on the hub's screen and Ethan stared up in amazement. Raq gazed down at Ethan, staring at his shoulder. A patch of brown rust had appeared on his pure white suit. He tried brushing it off, and as he did it began to grow bigger. It spread across his chest and his body began to disintegrate where the rust spread. "What…what is happening…Ronald…what is this…get it off me! Get it off me!!!"

"It's a virus Ethan," Raq said. "This time when I reentered my body I already knew that you were after me, and not killing off everyone in Elysium. I wasn't exactly sure why, so just to be safe I had Janu place a virus in my circuits. If any foreign consciousness was ever installed in my body, the virus would activate and the body would begin to self-destruct. I'm sorry Ethan. You see, people may be ignorant, but at the same time they have such great potential. You and I both remember the stricken world of the past and were afraid that it would return to that state. But people learn from their mistakes, Ethan. They want to change, they're trying to care for the planet more and all its treasures that it gives us so freely. If we just use the method you suggested it would be the same as going backwards. I want to move forward Ethan. I want to move forward to a world of real harmony where people nurture the earth, its animals and other people because they choose to and not because they were forced to."

"In this time since we separated Ethan, I've basically lived without a physical body. Most of the time people identify themselves with their bodies, but I've come to realize that the body is just a tool for this consciousness of ours. And our consciousness is such a rich and wonderful thing. It's full of feelings, and if we go deeper into it we find an ocean of tranquility. We connect to others through our consciousness even though they are not necessarily near us. Even now, I can feel my friends, outside this place, inside Elysium…there's no distance."

"And mortality, it isn't something we need to prevent, because our consciousness *is* immortal Ethan. It just goes on and on. I've experienced this and I'd hoped that you would too," Raq said as the rust reached Ethan's head.

"Ronald, you always were...a...real...drama queen," were the last words Ethan uttered as his form faded away.

Turning back to the hub, Raq started extracting instructions from Elysium's memory and decoding them. Then she began to execute her program. She was going to wake everyone in Elysium up. A screen unfolded and read, 'Initiate Sequence.' She hit the screen and activated the program. As she did, her own body started to glow the same ultra violet hue as the hub. She could feel herself being drawn into the hub. Her body was being broken up, separated into data and drawn into the CPU of Elysium. "How strange," she thought to herself, "In the end, the master key...was my own consciousness." And she was gone.

Xin Yu forced her eyes open. At first she couldn't see anything as her head was covered by a headset. Her arms were weak, frail things. She tried lifting them, but it was no use. Turning her body slightly, she felt her legs and arms tingling. A shot of pain wriggled up from her arm. It was the IV inserted into a vein at her wrist. After a few hours just lying there, she finally felt she had the strength to remove the headset. She removed it slowly, and light came piercing into her eyes. Everything was a blur, so she just sat there and let her eyes adjust to the light for a while. She could make out that she was in a small room. The IV in her arm hurt, but she didn't want to remove it yet. A terminal with a motion sensor was nearby and she could feel other tubes running between her legs. She decided to just sit and contemplate everything for a while, and her mind went back to those last moments in Elysium.

She'd been trying to convince everyone in Elysium that their world was just a virtual reality and that they were actually trapped within it. She'd used the link Raq had left her with to show everyone that she could just create things from thin air. She'd done all sorts of seemingly magical feats, explaining that this was all possible because they were really all jacked into a network. Some people believed her and she'd gained a following of sorts. There were people who wanted to act, who wanted to do something about it. So they started searching for information, anything that would lead them to more answers, but it was always shut off or access wasn't allowed. Eventually the gendarme had stepped in and she'd been locked up in detention for a while. One day, she suddenly found the door to her detention cell was open, and she stepped out and came to the lodge of the Detention Dome. On a large screen, she saw Rak's face. He looked different, violet purple streaks flowed from his blue hair and his eyes blazed yellow.

He spoke, "People of Elysium, recently you may have discovered that the world you exist in is a computerized one. I won't say it is not a real one, as I have existed in it before and have experienced very human things within this cyberspace. Your physical body is connected to this realm through a sensory headset, tubes and various equipment. There have been individuals outside of Elysium who have removed your memories and made you forget your previous selves. I will be restoring those memories slowly now and will gradually release the hold that keeps you in Elysium. Of course, Elysium will continue to exist as a place for people to come and interact and exchange with one another virtually. However it will no longer be able to be controlled by a single host, making any kind of mass control impossible. To do this I have entered the brain of Elysium and started programs which will eventually grant you your freedom. Those who wish to stay in this world must remember to maintain your physical bodies as I'm withdrawing the androids that have been keeping you entrapped in this state of amnesia for so long. However, they will provide care for you once you withdraw from

Elysium until your bodies have completely recovered. I hope that the same harmony I once saw in Elysium can be recreated outside of it on our own beautiful green planet. Farewell."

Phase Eighteen

No Distance

Chiyo noticed that the shouting and yelling had died down. Drew came to and was trying to stand up, but his leg needed treating.

"Just stay put Drew, I'm going to take a look," Chiyo said. Emerging in the corridor, Chiyo scanned up and down. The sounds of voices were getting further and further away. She slowly edged her way down the hallway, blaster in hand, and peeked around a nearby corner. Some troops were gathered there, she could just barely hear their voices.

"There's been no communication from command; everyone's just deserting their positions," one man's voice said.

"Yeah, they're saying Ethan and Colonel Joshua have been beaten. There's been no contact from them," another female voice cut in.

"I heard that the Front's got forces on the way here now! Everyone's deserted…we don't stand a chance!"

"Yeah, let's get out of here while we still can…"

The voices trailed off and Chiyo was wondering what the hell was going on. Had she done it? Had Raq won? She kept walking towards the main entrance, troopers were dropping their weapons and stripping off their uniforms all around her. They were just running off into the forest or taking flight suits, transports or anything they could get their hands on. The Puritanist army was running, dispersed, separating… finished. She came out of the barracks and into the sunshine. Just a short while ago, she'd wondered if she'd ever be able to see the light of the sun again. But here she was, basking in its healing rays. Squinting, she could see aircraft and flight suits closing in. As they approached, she could make out the Front's markings on them. Elation filled her entire being. Her thoughts turned to

Raq, the most selfless human that she'd ever met, who'd lost her humanity a long time ago. Tears filled her eyes as she silently thanked her. "Where are you now Raq?" she wondered.

"The world needs its idealists," thought Joshua as he slowly walked through the cool forest. "Ethan failed because he wasn't thorough enough. He was always too emotional." Joshua heard the sounds of flight suits and aircraft overhead. The Puritanits were through. "It doesn't matter," he mused. Joshua had his own plans and his own schemes. All he needed was time. In time he would make them come true. "The world needs idealists," he kept thinking as he trudged through the mire of the forest, hidden from the sun. "Yes, idealists are what make the world go round."

It had already been three months since she'd woken up from the dream that had been Elysium. Xin Yu had always used her real name, so that didn't change. In reality, she had long black hair too, but her eyes were a matching deep black color. The strength had returned to her body, but not to her heart. A part of her heart remained in Elysium, with the man she loved. Placing her bag over her shoulder, she wiped tears from her eyes as she got into the transport that would take her away from the colony she'd been staying in. The driver wasn't an android but a man wearing the Front's uniform and sunglasses. He smiled at her as he took a seat at the wheel. Xin Yu's heart skipped several beats when she saw that smile. He had short wavy brown hair, he wasn't as tall, and he didn't dress like him...but...that smile.

The man started the transport and turned around. He removed his sunglasses to reveal his shimmering brown eyes. They shone, just like...an android's. "Where to ma'am?" he asked. She didn't know what to say all of a sudden. The way he moved, his smile, could it possibly be? "If you don't tell me soon Xin Yu, I'll have to..."

Rak felt two warm arms around him, and the emotion of the embrace seeped into him and filled him up. He felt joyful tears touch his neck and brought Xin Yu's head up to look at her. He'd never seen her before, yet he had always felt her. In all this time his heart had never left her side.

"Rak," she said...

Her lips touched his and even though he was just a human consciousness in an android body, he thought, "There was never any distance between us at all."

The End

www.ingramcontent.com/pod-product-compliance
Ingram Content Group UK Ltd.
Pitfield, Milton Keynes, MK11 3LW, UK
UKHW020127250726
13967UKWH00002B/513

9 781300 123781